PRAISE FOR *THE RIVER KNOWS MY NAME*

"Mortada Gzar's utterly appealing and original protagonist Charlotte, daughter of archetypal Father Emmo, also a physician, will captivate any reader. Gzar describes her inner world with a sharp eye for emotional detail. He is skilled at characterizing the unpredictable mix of magical thinking and cool realism that only precocious, observant children can possess. Charlotte's recklessness, charm, and attachments pull at us. This is a novel in which emotional delicacy and comic absurdity meld seamlessly: signs of loneliness appear on a girl's fingernails, and a small figurine of Baby Jesus is stolen repeatedly. Characters such as deputy vice consuls, handsome idlers, saints, guards, and ghosts all play their parts in Charlotte's world. Gzar presents an unforgettable girl, a kind of stranger in a strange land, who is gifted with abundant imagination, depth of feeling, and a fearlessness we all might envy."

—Sun Yung Shin, poet and author of *The Wet Hex*

"The fifth novel from award-winning Iraqi novelist, filmmaker, and visual artist Mortada Gzar is a sweeping, impassioned work of delirium and history that is also a stunning evocation of—and homage to—the natural world of the Iraqi marshes. Transporting us from the American Christian missions to the British colonial enterprise to the internal migrations in the ethnically—and religiously—diverse nascent nation-state of Iraq at the turn of the twentieth century, *The River Knows My Name* is a literary tour de force, unfolding through the sheer power of language a world alongside ours—vast, delirious, teeming with free and wild associations, magnificently inventive, and mostly invisible to us otherwise."

—Yasmeen Hanoosh, literary translator, author, and critic

THE RIVER KNOWS MY NAME

THE RIVER KNOWS MY NAME

MORTADA GZAR

TRANSLATED BY LUKE LEAFGREN

Translated from Arabic by Luke Leafgren.

Published by Amazon Crossing, Seattle

www.apub.com

ISBN-13: 9781542038966 (hardcover)
ISBN-13: 9781542038973 (paperback)
ISBN-13: 9781542038997 (digital)

Cover design by David Drummond
Cover image: © LuisPortugal, © thomas porter / 500px / Getty

Printed in the United States of America

To the Iraqi people of the marshlands.
To Father Wanis, founder of the Rajaa Upper School in Basra.
And to Gavin Maxwell, who wrote about the Iraqi otter, on the verge of extinction, and also to his friend Mijbil.

Night descends again; the city drinks it
Deep, as do the passersby, like a sad song.
Street lamps ignite like oleander blossoms;
Like Medusa's eyes, they petrify every heart with weakness,
Like a vow proclaiming fire to the people of Babylon.

—Badr Shakir al-Sayyab, from "The Blind Prostitute"

During his time among the Marsh Arabs, Maxwell acquired Mijbil, the first of his famous otters. Mijbil belonged to a race previously unknown to science.

—From Ring of Bright Water and Beyond

AUTHOR'S NOTE

This story is the product of the author's imagination, and the characters are not drawn from real individuals, nor is it a historical documentary. Nevertheless, in order to avoid ambiguity, the names of imaginary characters have been changed, along with the rivers and places around them, to other imaginary names.

THE FIRST QUARTER

RUNNING AWAY FROM HOME ON A GRAPE LEAF

If otters could read, my life in this city would have been far easier.

Every night, I can still hear the crows drumming their beaks against the hull of our upturned boat. I was ten-plus-four years old at the time. Since I was a child, I've always liked transforming my age into a mathematical equation. The first number is the age I'd like to be; the rest, after the *plus*, is unimportant, and people don't remember the second number like they do the first when I tell them my age like this. (I didn't know that would help me later to reduce the cruelty of getting older and to increase or decrease the ages of the people around me however I wished.) At any given moment, my father could be forty-plus-ten years old or forty-five-plus-three months, depending on my mood.

Now I'm fifteen-plus-sixty years old. I was a child when this story took place, and because of it, I have remained a child. I have memorized all its details to the point that I can tell them in the dark. That's because I never stop recounting it to children. That's why I must remind myself that today, I'm telling it to adults, not to children.

I had just one name, Charlotte, and I was the daughter of Father Emmanuel, the doctor. I had traveled with him to Basra, where the people called him Father Emmo. In the first weeks, before I got used to the name of the city, I carried a map of the world with me wherever I went, with the names of countries, coastlines, and gulfs. One time, when my father was distracted while setting a patient's broken fingers, I stole his telescope and slipped out onto the balcony. I raised it up, searching the sky for the name of that city. I was certain that if I only looked closely or used a large enough telescope, the letters of its big name would appear in the air, just like on my map. I nearly caught the name among the clouds, written by a flock of cormorants, and would have done so had my father not snatched the telescope out of my hands. Picking me up with his rough fingers, he laid me across his shoulder and carried me off like a rolled-up carpet. When he set me down on the bed, I understood what I had to do. I raised my right leg off the floor and pointed it toward the horizon so that he could attach my left leg, the artificial one, and make sure they were both the same length. That way, I would not be embarrassed by limping or making an annoying knocking sound when I walked.

According to the schedule attached to the windowpane, I would get my artificial leg for five hours that day because it was a Friday. My father drew up a strict table of the appointed times to attach the leg and to take it off. He drafted the plan in a pretty turquoise-blue ink that turned yellow after being scorched by the summer sun. Then it faded completely after one short winter. I knew that betraying the schedule was the worst thing I could do with respect to the authority that Father Emmo asserted over my leg. Neglecting our agreement meant he would become angry. But that sentence contains an impossibility. No one had ever seen my father get angry. Instead, he would always suppress his anger, and his tone of voice would adopt a melodic softness that drew me inexorably toward him. I always found that tedious and annoying, harder than if I were to actually see him become angry. I don't know why. I wish I could deny that the emotions I feel are somewhat complicated, but that is how it is.

Father Emmo, the preacher and the bone-setting doctor who treated dysentery and fever in a hospital for the strangers who fell asleep on the banks of the Shatt like bloated whales, gave me the leg every day at the appointed time so that I could walk. He would lean over so far that I could see the green and purple veins behind his ears. Bending his knee a little, he took the leg out of my hand. Moving his right foot back slightly to brace himself, he pressed the prosthetic leg against my stump, as though he were putting a slipper onto Cinderella's foot. He handled it like a newborn baby, patting its back to put it to sleep as it rejoined my body. I disliked the ritual so much. I could only see it as a leg of presumably high-quality rubber, aged like wine for decades in a medical storeroom. It was one of four thousand legs made in the days of the Civil War for a short soldier, who had engraved his name upon it: THIS IS THE LEG OF SOLDIER CORBIN O'HARO. THANK YOU. Then he sold it.

I decided I would leave. I would escape the cage of solicitude and seek an adventure on my own. I tried that first by breaking out of the schedule. When the time came to take off my leg to hang it in the sun and sterilize it, I hid. That broke the schedule and won me more time with my leg as people searched for me. But I was not patient enough to do that for more than a few minutes, and I did not succeed in abolishing the schedule entirely. I dreamed of leaving my room, which was attached to the hospital, and walking along the river, following its course without it being aware of me. I had heard from the Indian nurses that this river followed its winding path after being born from the union of the Tigris and Euphrates. From that point, it was called the One-Eyed Tigris. I longed to see it and to understand how a river could be born with just one eye. I felt that the river hid its childhood from me, just as I hid the curiosity I felt for rivers. The river was jealous of me; I actually thought that. I paced back and forth in the hallway before approaching the vestibule where my father stood on the threshold. I attracted his gaze by walking with slow, halting steps as I followed a convoy of ants moving in a big circular route, ignoring all the cracks in the wall. I confirmed that I was there with him, as always, and I had no intention to move any farther away. I was playing in a safe environment under his eyes.

A ladybug landed on my hand, red with black spots. My father bobbed his head as he called to me, "Eight?" He repeated the question, in all seriousness. He wanted to know whether the ladybug had eight spots on its wings. He knew there were only seven, not eight. He had previously made a wager with me that if I found a ladybug with eight spots, he would stand upside down on his hands. It was an old promise, going back to the days when I was a little child and he had the goal of teaching me to count.

I smiled at him. "Seven." Seven, like usual. Seven, and I had no hope that there would ever be eight black dots on the wings of the ladybug, but I would count them as often as he asked.

I returned to my room, where I put a woolen jacket over my shoulders that made me look like a ram that had gotten lost. The hour of flight was imminent. I entered my father's room. The smell of his clothes, spread over the bed, stung my nose. I wanted to escape that smell, so I opened the window, and a hornet slipped into the room. First, I needed to pack a canvas sack with copies of the Gospels, many of them. I found them in my father's drawer, set into the wall, in all their holy number. Before he returned to practice medicine here, my father had been a minister who brought people the good news of Jesus. The Reformed Church of New York had sent him to the Arabian Peninsula in order to reform the sons of Ishmael and "return them to the Lord's flock." He settled in Basra and made multiple trips to Najd, Yemen, and Oman, though he focused his activities here. He rode around in a boat built locally, carved with the heads of lions and lambs, and he spoke to the fishermen in a refined Arabic about the miracles of the Holy King. They gaped in astonishment. Then they burst into tears and wet their sleeves with snot. Before he had finished recounting Jesus's miracles when He appeared to the monks in the mountain, they chanted in unison, "O God! Grant prayers and peace upon Mohammed and Mohammed's family!" They were fully convinced my father was speaking about Mohammed, not about Jesus, and he spent no effort to correct the flow of stories that inspired those mistaken feelings. It was clear that it was no use trying to change their minds.

I would see him throw his enormous body onto the bed at the end of the night after returning the sack of Gospels to their drawer. He carried it out heavy and brought it back heavy. Not a single Gospel had been sold. Then he began snoring. Sometimes it reminded me of a train whistle, and sometimes of a ship's horn, especially when he returned from preaching among the dockworkers. I would strip off his jacket and pull the folded fabric out from under him.

Little by little, he returned to the practice of medicine. He despaired of people's moods and his ability to change them from Mohammedans into followers of Jesus. He took up medicine again and all its aspects, prepared to treat everyone who sought out Strangers Hospital, which he had founded with two former nuns.

The illnesses of the strangers who visited the city or stopped there were as strange as they were. "They've composed their illnesses out of themselves," he used to say. He didn't hesitate to treat anyone, even those who suffered pains that were impossible to locate in their bodies, like those who came to him complaining of forgetfulness, sluggishness, and desire. He would work with each for a long time, perhaps because they had no choice but to listen to him prattle on with sermons and lessons. But in the end, his words were a scandal, and his compassionate exhortations were no longer suitable for his white apron, stained with blood and antiseptics. His despair intensified, but then he renewed his belief that treating the broken, the blind, and the broken-spirited was a very Christlike act. Preaching the Gospel might mean healing the bodies of people too. He grew excited and wrote a telegram to his colleagues, scattered across the Mohammedan countries, as much to alert them as to remind himself and anchor his thoughts, which were proven by a line from the Epistle of James: "Not many of you should become teachers, my brothers." A Christian preacher here or there among these people might be enough. But he was a preacher with his scalpel, his stethoscope, and the spool of silken thread that he used to sew up the wounds of the Mohammedans.

All his tools were hidden in that drawer. I opened it and plunged inside. I passed into his hidden world where he hid his shawl, his statue, and his Gospels. The odor of incense buried there months ago emanated. The piles of books tottered as I drew the Gospels from the bottom. I opened some of them and smelled the piercing scent. I shut my eyes and felt I was flying among the winged words of God. These editions, skillfully printed in Malta under my father's supervision, used warm Arabic letters fresh from the furnaces of the translating priests, and they exhaled the perfume of roses and mint oil when you flipped through their pages. I filled my bag with some of them and paused before I left that room knowing I was leaving it for the last time. I would be stepping outside that world and closing the door behind me. It was hard for me to deny the statue of Baby Jesus, who was directing his gaze toward me, boring his innocent eyes deep into mine. I felt his need to escape, like me, or his desire not to let me go on my adventure alone. Despite the age gap between us, I understood him, and I did not make him plead for long. I stuffed him among my stolen goods and hurried out.

In the blink of an eye, I had descended to the lower floor. It was my father's busiest hour, the time when he placed his head against the chests of the elderly and asked them to take a deep breath. I shot past like an arrow without him seeing me. I wrapped myself in a woman's black abaya, a game I learned from the little Arab girls who came to the hospital with their mothers and played tricks by disappearing within the abayas and waving their arms as though rowing oars through the waves of soft black fabric. That small sea helped me reach the gate, and from there to the end of the wooden bridge, which was a bridge unlike any other: two bowed palm trees extending horizontally and connecting the two shoulders of a small stream that had branched off from the

One-Eyed Tigris. I did not have a fixed direction in mind, but my head had become a compass needle, trembling and spinning toward flight.

I was, I am, and I will continue to be enthralled by that enticing notion found in stories of monks fleeing the world. That's what set my compass of flight dancing, and my imagination would run between the steppes, the hills, and the valleys. In my mind, I lived among the beasts and the crows, their beaks stained with blood and insect wings. I fled the world and became a holy woman, so shaken by the fear of God that all feared me, even the lions, foxes, and giant snakes. No one knew me, while I knew nothing but Jesus's shadows. I would follow in his footsteps no matter what befell me. I would feel pain, hunger, thirst, and fatigue. I would carry an invisible cross, under which my desires slept forever. To tell the truth, I did not fully realize that what I was doing was escaping my father and running away. Something more than a desire to run away moved me. Perhaps it was my longing to see God, or at least to plunge into some adventure, marvelous and miraculous, the kind you read about in children's books even though they do not actually happen to anyone. No, I cannot deny that I was deeply affected by those small books, their pages brown as corn bread, which contained biographies of the monks in the deserts of Egypt, the mountains of Lebanon, and the heights over the Tigris and Euphrates. I never spoke openly to my father about that inclination toward renunciation and leaving the world. I knew he would be angry and would place my insistent feelings under close observation for a week. He would breathe over my head so that the spiritual notions and the doves of that mood would fly away.

I ran away. Yes, Charlotte ran away.

I felt the weight of the bag as I crossed the stream. It grew heavier with every step, and its handle was turning into a blade that cut my fingers. The statue of Baby Jesus found a window for his head in the opening of the bag, and I thought it was becoming fatter, its cheeks bloated and heavy. When I reached the bank of the large river, I was nearly overcome by alarm. The rivermen were competing for me and waving with their oars. Four boats had gathered below me, their pointed prows banging into each other. I chose a yellow one, dyed with henna, in which sat a woman, who let the wind billow through her abaya as though it were a black sail. I thought the boat was traveling with her alone until her son emerged from the water, and the boat rocked us back and forth as he pulled himself into it. The eyes of Baby Jesus drew him, and he began examining the statue and stroking its head. I told them I wanted to go to the other bank. The boy set his oar against a willow trunk and pushed off, sending the boat backward toward the middle of the Shatt. I noticed his mother smiling as she observed him set to work in earnest. The boy rowed and turned his face toward his mother. "Look at me, rowing as skillfully as the grown-ups!" he told her with his eyes. Then he focused his gaze on picking out a path between the fishing nets and the nearby boats.

The boat was not slender like the others. I felt I was sitting on a grape leaf. The palm trees began obscuring my father's hospital. It grew smaller and smaller on the horizon as we rocked atop the water. The mother, who had temples covered with tattoos and a gold ring hanging from her nose, yawned and dozed off. She woke up and then rested her tired head on the gunwale of the boat. A gust of wind roused her by filling her abaya with air. She told me this was the first day for her son, Finjan, to work on board the boat of his father, who had been taken away by soldiers one year before in order to fight for the Turks in the Caucasus. The woman turned every which way like a frightened dove as she drew a small onion from her lap. She tied the onion to a delicate cloth ribbon. Then she produced another onion and attached it to the ribbon. The boat was rocking, and its near collisions with boats around it made my heart race, but looking at the mother as she made that necklace of onions calmed my anxiety. She watched the boat's progress and distributed her glances between me, Finjan, and the onion necklace. After finishing the necklace, she rocked it like a swing. She stood up and walked toward Finjan, not caring that she was rocking the boat. Her thick shadow washed over the entire boat, some of it even falling onto the water. She smiled bashfully as she placed the necklace around his neck and said to me, "I circumcised him yesterday." Then she lifted his robe to reveal his bloody privates, wrapped in a bandage and looking to me like the head of a hooded vulture. The boy was irritated, and he pushed his robe back down. A flock of nightingales passed by, shooting between and around us like arrows. Going back to her seat, his mother told him, "The onions will ease the pain of your little nightingale."

A few minutes passed before the boy recovered his dignity, at which point I came to know what his mother had meant by the nightingale. Finjan became more energetic and lighter when he felt his mother's eyes watching him, as though she were hot rays that burned the hair on his head. He even began to swing his chest right and left to strike the onions with his nipples. He pulled back his lips to reveal teeth stained by lemon-and-cinnamon tea. Laughing, he gave himself a shake, making his cheeks tremble in an alternating motion with his large belly. We were about to reach the heart of the river. He was rowing and contending with the adult boatmen. He struck the waves just like they did. I did not laugh, nor did I feel any delight. My eyes were frozen. I bowed my head and felt my insides contract. I was afraid to look back in case I caught a glimpse of Strangers Hospital, or even my father himself chasing me aboard another boat, eyes flashing with anger and concern, as the people around him shouted to one another and composed their exclusive story: "Father Emmo is pursuing his fleeing daughter!" Running at their head would be the two nuns who worked as nurses, making the sign of the cross and stumbling over hospital sheets as they called my name. But none of that happened.

I raised my hand and pointed a bent finger forward. "I want to go there," I told Finjan. This "there" meant the place where the two rivers came together and gave birth to the One-Eyed Tigris, that short green river. The boy pressed his lips together before swearing to me that he needed to double the distance he had traveled in order for "there" to turn into "here." Without warning, the boat lurched violently. The bag containing the Gospels was overturned, and Baby Jesus was dumped out onto his face, as though trying to crawl for the first time. When Finjan bent over to pick up the statue, it was no secret that the wooden Jesus with the black-lined eyes had aroused the boy and his mother's curiosity. I recovered my composure and said a prayer of thanks to God.

THE ROOM OF SHADOWY LIGHT

A convoy of boats passed by, carrying piles of clouds. At first, I didn't know why the women around us hid their faces when the clouds went by. Finjan said, "This is cotton on the way to the dyers." In those days, no one could match my poetic imagination, which emanated from my mind with the pungency of vinegar. Everything around me seemed like a poem. I saw the cotton as clouds, the trunks of palm trees as stork legs.

A small boat crossed in front of us, only large enough for one rower, who lifted his oars to splash water and moss down Finjan's neck. "They're taking the cotton to the church, not to the dyers," he corrected. The word *church* rang in my ears, spinning like a coin. I spread my arms as though to fly through the clouds to the altar of the Son of God. My young soul was covered by that cotton, which looked like lambswool. Lambs were, according to my father's explanations, the sign for all Jesus's loved ones. All of us were lambs, even if wool did not tumble over our bodies, and even if one of us was an insane girl—someone just like me—entranced by the idea of running away from home.

The cotton boats were still passing by as we reached a crowded intersection where boats diverged along the dikes and pools of water. Once again I saw the women wrapped in black covering their faces in shame when the cotton boats passed. Indeed, some of the men rowing the boats bowed their heads when the cotton passed. Finally, I understood that this cotton was meant for women to use during their monthly period. But I ignored that as I coughed and blew my nose, reacting to the cotton dust that was a gift from the Good Shepherd. I heard snatches of conversation from the boatmen around me, saying that hundreds of women, refugees from the war in the north and Armenian women fleeing the massacres, came down this river, the Shatt. The wife of Kadhim Pasha, who was the provincial governor known as the wali, was gathering cotton, gifts, aid, and clothes for these women.

I loosened the strap of my leg a little and lifted my dress to air out that plastic part of my body. I had exceeded the schedule now, and it was time to return the leg to my father. It was exactly the moment when my father would enter my room to reclaim the artificial leg and let my stump rest. He would be knocking on the door to my room, holding the cotton towel, the bandages, and the alcohol. He would separate me from my leg and let me sleep or memorize hymns while he disinfected my festering body. Then he would place the leg across his shoulder and leave. I thought about all his probable reactions. All his gifts of kindness and poise would not heal his heart from the severe bruise of my running away. Some hours later, he would discover that the leg was missing, for Charlotte—your celebrated correspondent in these lines—decided to kidnap her leg and disappear with it entirely. My father had accompanied me from Seattle to save me from the typhoid fever, which had started to steal out through prison windows and find its way to the church steeples, and now he set a precise schedule for my leg to protect the stump from decay and restricted blood circulation. But I finally succeeded in slipping away. My father liked to call me his cherry blossom, and now the wind had carried me away. Despite all the tribulations and punishments, and after trying and failing four times, my fifth attempt had succeeded. That's what I told myself, enunciating the big words calmly in my mind—only for a shorebird to poop on my head in that very moment. Finjan turned his face away but could not stifle the sound of his laughter.

◆ ◆ ◆

Even if I forget everything else, I'll never forget the smell that would burn the angels' noses from its intensity. It happened when we passed a narrow harbor where passengers were boarding other boats to carry them off into the distance. Every oar in the river slowed as necks craned to stare at the source of the odor: a great dead whale that the men were towing toward the land. Its odor refused to adhere to the carcass. Inside its half-open mouth, a dozen children were pinching their noses closed or covering them with their hands as they danced and sang. Finjan said this whale had lost its way in the sea and turned into the river, where it suffocated in the brackish water. "Every year, a whale loses its way and enters the city without its soul."

The boy's mother rose and enfolded both of us inside her abaya, creating a layer of insulation from the polluted air that was far more effective than a wall of massive stones. Entering the mother's clothes seemed like going inside a wooden camera box, just as photographers do when they hide their faces under those black curtains. Finjan talked and laughed and plugged his nostrils, even as he continued to row us from where we sat underneath the abaya. I asked myself what the Lord meant by this message. What did it mean for me to see a dead whale with little children playing inside its mouth, which hung open like a cloth doll's? I could not say, and I did not arrive at any answer in that moment. Not all of the Lord's messages have something to say. Perhaps He was joking with me, getting a good laugh as He peered down from His throne, cleaning His fingernails of a story He had only that instant finished writing for me. I pondered the significance of what awaited me in the book of fate, along with other stories that were stamped with disappointments and difficulties that far exceeded a perished whale.

The boy's mother asked me where I was going. I merely took out the statue of Baby Jesus, embraced it, and put it back in its place. We were rowing through a palm forest, where the grasses took on every shade of green. I began reviewing this foolish adventure of mine and how easy it had been for me to run away. Then the boat crashed into a wooden piling, startling me from my reverie. It appeared as though we had arrived. But where? I did not know. Yet the boy and his mother decided we were there. Finjan planted his oar into the edge of the bank. He jumped out before me and reached out his hand to help me clamber onto the dry ground while his mother placed her hand on my back to support me. As the boy handed me my sackcloth bag, he cried, "Where is the kohl-eyed toy?" referring to Baby Jesus. Hearing him, I patted down my entire body. I could not accept the idea of losing the statue. I jumped back into the boat and lifted up the damp mats covering the hull. I opened the folds of the mother's abaya in case Jesus had slipped into the room of shadow and light. I stuck my head in and pulled it out again, with odors of musk and frankincense clinging to it. I lifted up other parts of the boat's floor. I plugged my nose to ward off the stench of dung that was stirred up in the bowels of the vessel. I leaned my head over the side and studied the surface of the water, but all I saw was my troubled face staring back.

Finjan reached out his hand a second time and brought me out of the river. I took two steps onto land and sat in the lap of a palm tree. I turned right and left, peering among the trunks of the palms in case Baby Jesus was soaring off somewhere or was hanging in the interlaced palm fronds. Maybe he had decided to go on ahead to the path, leading the way for me on my journey. I'm not joking: I really thought that way. And it seemed that Finjan was even more earnest than me in his surprise and distress. He came over to me and placed his palm on my head. I may have been a little older than him, but in that moment, he was older than me by fifty years—or five-plus-fifty. He promised me he would find the statue and bring it back to me, mentioning some of the possibilities that had come into his head and crowded out his memory of his foreskin being cut off on the previous night. He told me that one of the rowers may have stolen it when we weren't watching, and he asked me to wait and not to budge from my spot until he returned.

I went on watching the scene around me. It was not obvious that the river was born in that spot. I needed to fly up in a hot-air balloon or on a magic broom to ascertain the precise moment it poured out between the legs of the two tributary rivers, the Tigris and the Euphrates. They gave birth to it shamefacedly, hidden there among the palm trunks and mounds of mud, and ruined my pleasure. I guessed that Finjan would not return. His mother would not allow him to waste time on a strange foreign girl looking for her doll. I closed my bag, hiding the Gospels from sight. Everyone around me was rowing, and I felt the small island itself swaying underneath me.

I awoke from that daydream to the sound of a man striking a drum and saying, "Read the *Harbor* newspaper! Four pages more delicious than sesame bread! Don't stop until you reach the very end!" Three slaves carried bundles of newspapers. They moved in time to the beat of the drummer, who did not stop reciting his pitch until the moment he jumped into the boat. The voice of the drummer faded as he receded in the distance, and I focused my eyes upon him, expecting Finjan to appear from that same direction. In the following minutes, I noticed that the roads were many and that this river afflicted the land with hundreds of streams. I turned my head, examining all the routes from which the boy might appear.

Then, upon the very edge of despair, Baby Jesus suddenly appeared, just as He always did.

At first, I did not understand. Embarrassed and rueful, Finjan's mother opened my sackcloth bag and returned Baby Jesus to his place. She carefully closed it as she murmured an apology. After loosening her veil and revealing the decorative tattoos of vegetable ink that covered half her face like beads, she bent down to kiss and caress the bag. Then she stuck her hand inside her robe to anoint her breasts with the statue's oil, seeking its blessing. She closed her eyes and let out a wail. "Finjan ought to fall at your feet and apologize," she said. "That's the least he can do. If only he would! But his head is dry as wood." As she said *wood*, she pointed to the head of the statue.

I didn't utter a word. I was too busy hugging the bag, delighted by what had happened. Finjan and his mother turned away from me and set off. I was bubbling over with curiosity over why they had done it, but I managed to extinguish the thought and forgive them. I caught up to them and asked about the road that led north. Finjan's mother told her son to take me to the nearby port where large round boats embarked for the lakes, from which I could get out halfway there. Then she jumped like a water nymph into another boat and disappeared. The mother thought I was on my way home to my family's palace along the banks of the river. She imagined I was a daughter of the great and mighty, or at least a daughter of someone employed in the service of the wali, which is the word used for the governor of the province, and that it would be easy for me to board one of those boats and then get off again before it disappeared into the reed forests.

The hour of sunset gripped my breath, and fear began creeping into my chest. The sun had not yet fully set, but my heart, which had naked devils dancing upon it, was struck by a fierce wretchedness. It was the same thing I felt whenever the sun went down and my father was still downstairs at Strangers Hospital, and I gnawed on the wood of the window because I was so bored while waiting for him.

Choking on a sob, I said to Finjan, "Take me home!" I struck my chest with my palm. I slapped my forehead and then the ground. I jumped to my feet and began rocking the boat back and forth as I screamed at him, "I want my father!" I screamed it in Arabic, in English, and in broken Assyrian. "I'm not from here," I said. "Take Jesus and the Gospels, and bring me home right now." I grabbed my braids and pulled them upward. This behavior was extremely foolish and bizarre, but it succeeded in frightening him, especially after I yelled at him, "Now! Now! I beg you, my good sir!"

"Get in and hold on tight," said Finjan. "Don't frighten me! I'm scared too. People will think I'm trying to hurt you. Be quiet! Be quiet!" Then, when he saw that I had become calm and obedient, wiping my nose and drying my tears, he exerted his verbal control over me, saying, "Shut your mouth, you speckled whore. I'm bringing you back to your family." By *speckled*, he was referring to the freckles on my face.

All that happened quickly. He pushed the boat with excessive lightness, skillfully avoiding a collision with the other boats and their owners, whose curiosity impelled them to approach us and ask each other what all the commotion was about. One of them threw a dried ear of corn at us, which fell at our feet.

When the prodigious mass of Strangers Hospital came into view, I sighed deeply and turned toward Finjan. Unaware I was watching, he wiped his forehead, which was slick with sweat. My face showed remorse, though I didn't actually say anything. For his part, his anger had subsided, and he began to release the words that had been bottled up in his throat. They all came out more easily after he had delivered me to the harbor, set me on the slippery hill, and pushed off with his oar, as lightly as a tiger tamer. As he moved away in his boat, he waved at me and, by way of apology for stealing the statue and returning it, said, "Forgive me! I saw Abdullah in your bag and said, 'Here he is, adjuring me.'"

As Finjan had seen it, the statue was of Abdullah, the son of Prophet Mohammed's grandson. I wanted to correct him and explain that this was Baby Jesus, but my voice seemed soft compared to his passionate enthusiasm as he went on to say, "I promised Abdullah I would teach him how to steer the boat, how to hunt redfish with a spear, and how to spit in the air without getting your own face wet. I took him from your bag and stuffed him inside the net we use to catch shrimp. I dried him off really good after that, and I heard him crying from the soap. I told him, 'I won't get the soap in your eyes, Abdullah!'"

Even though I felt it would accomplish nothing, I told him this was Jesus, not Abdullah. He paid no attention to my words and concluded by saying, "Where did you buy that leg? Are you selling it? Maybe a trade for this basket of shrimp? A basket of shrimp and dates, and you give me Infant Abdullah and your leg? The soldiers conscripted my father five times. The first time, he came home after cutting off his pointer finger so he couldn't shoot a gun, but they came to get him again. Then he cut off his foot in order to get out of it. But they took him back anyway. He put rat poison on his eyes and went half-blind, but they still took him away. If he comes back, he'd be so happy about that leg. Do you really need it?"

I was too busy gathering up my things to listen to him. He was rowing away, getting smaller and smaller until he disappeared behind a palm tree that had grown in the shape of a P, toppled over and plunging its head in the water.

Two days before that futile journey, a boat of Indians and Arabs had passed behind the hospital. They set up a statue of Abdullah, son of the Prophet's grandson. It was a little smaller than the statue of Baby Jesus, and it may have been a stick or a bundle of rags and not a carved statue. They wrapped it in green silk, surrounded it with candles and sticks of incense. They honored it by reciting the name of Infant Abdullah, who was shot with an arrow by enemies more than a thousand years ago and died in his father's arms, crying from his thirst, after the poison-tipped weapon had pierced his neck. From the kitchen of the hospital's pharmacy, I watched my father walk with them, sometimes imitating them by putting a handful of dirt from the road on his head, crying and striking his chest, having torn open his shirt. That was before the wali's men raided the street to drive away the festive gathering and restore the street's typical fear. When I asked my father what it all meant, he said that even the fish cry for that poor infant, just as the Indians and Arabs, and it's because of these tears that the sea is salty. Every year, mothers celebrate the anniversary of his death. Most likely, Finjan had spoken to the statue when I wasn't looking. Perhaps he saw his mother entreating it, asking it to grant her wishes. If I were in his position, I would have made the same mistake between Baby Jesus and the child of the Prophet's grandson. He vowed to teach it how to row a boat if it healed him from the wound of his circumcision. When he saw it with me, he stole it, and when his circumcision healed, he felt that the statue had fulfilled its promise, so he returned it to me.

That was not the source of my greatest anguish that day. After Finjan disappeared from sight, I turned to see how I could quickly reach Strangers Hospital, and how I might keep myself from collapsing in tears at my father's feet so that he would forgive me, and how instead I would fake tears paired with pride so that he would not speak harshly with me. The most important thing was that the leg of Soldier Corbin would help me get there. I urged myself on, studying the horizon and the gray hospital. I had taken only a few steps when I knelt down on one knee. The light of the sun reached my eyes as they swam with tears. I was in the wrong spot. I had indicated to Finjan that this was the hospital, and he followed my lead. Would that he hadn't! It was only another building that looked like the hospital: the color was the same, the smell of the Shatt was the same, but there were fewer people . . . I tried to look more closely. I stared in every direction. But nothing changed. I was still lost, in the literal meaning of the word. Along with that heavy feeling of dismay, a delicate layer of joy seemed to settle upon me. At least, that is my explanation now, as I recall that day decades later. It was the kind of delight at slipping away that might be felt by a grape that has swung a long time without falling from its bunch. The grape cries from the pain of dropping, but it enjoys the energy of rolling free.

The time had come to try my usual trick. If you ask me how I learned it, I'll tell you it was from children's church in Washington, but I long felt that it was my own private trick, something I invented for myself—or rather, something that the Lord laid in my path. What it comes down to is that whenever I'm uncertain about something, I open the Gospel and place it at the base of a tree. Then I let the wind play upon its pages until they open at some page. I approach, give thanks to God, and read the two open pages to find some testimony or indication or solution or path or direction. So that's what I did. I opened the bag and leaned Baby Jesus against a tree. I spread all the Gospels out in front of me. The collective space they took up was like a musical band. The wind ought to serve as the divine conductor, guiding every page to play an unequivocal answer. Did that actually happen? I waited around a quarter hour, but the pages of the Gospels did not move. They did not fold or make the slightest sound. The Gospels remained just as they were, on the pages where I had opened them, as though telling me, "It's up to you."

SUNS IN A PIGGY BANK

Everyone I met in those days is like a marble column erected in the deserts of my memory. Other people pass before me. They grow larger and smaller, they die and dissolve, while those columns battle the winds of exposure and poison. They have still not passed from my mind. They sit in my memory like Babylonian temples, while others, all those that came after them, fade away like a blown dandelion.

The sun was burning me, and hot stones seared the sole of my foot. The cawing of the larks announced that I was lost. That was the moment I met Shathra.

Shathra. Articulating the first syllable of her name was like half an attempt at a hiss. The correct pronunciation was achieved when you actually did that—hiss, I mean—and then caught yourself before people began making fun of you. As for the rest of her name, it slips and slides from under your tongue, tumbling down to your feet.

I was tired from walking and circling the building that looked like Strangers Hospital. I walked, approaching it from the shore and stopping every now and then to pull a thorn out of the sole of my foot. I threw myself down, stretching out on the sloping bank. My foot touched the water and was refreshed by the cool current of the Shatt. I was so tired that I began to doze off. A small wave began lapping against my artificial leg. I felt a light tickle. The cold water stole into the hollow of the prosthetic and flooded me with a refreshing pleasure. I fell into a deep sleep and woke up without my leg. I uprooted a tall reed and began hobbling along as quickly as I could, following the surface of the river in search of my leg. The river split into four separate channels. I followed the largest of them as it wound around a palm tree with a curved back. An otter jumped up to my chest and wriggled its way into my clothes. Plunging down my neckline, it emerged from the bottom of my dress, as though it were used to swimming through girls' bodies. That's when I saw her, Shathra, though I didn't know her name yet. She sat cross-legged, as erect and square as a cubed die. Beside her rose a column of bricks, crowned by stones that were inscribed with an Arabic script of intertwined letters, their heads and tails wrestling together. Perhaps it was a tomb.

She had been charged with searching for me, and she had found me with the help of one of her otters. She had perceived my breath, mixed with sobs, and approached me from behind. Catching me off guard, she threw herself on top of me with a single sinuous jump. She was thinking like a fishhook and made herself into the bait that drew me in.

When she was sure she had me under control, she said, "Your father is searching for you. We should hurry back."

She felt me resisting and fighting back in her arms. I cursed her with words she didn't understand. Her solidity was exactly what was necessary to persuade my stubbornness to submit. I collapsed beneath her and vowed I would go with her, but that I would not return without Soldier Corbin's leg. I raised my dress for her so she could see the amputated stump. Then a fit of coughing came over me, so violent that my chest nearly exploded.

At that moment, the heads of nearly twenty otters emerged from the grass. The scene did not frighten me so much as it delighted me. Shathra remained where she was, sprawled across me and pinning my whole body down like a paperweight in my father's office. She raised her face slowly when white smoke stole along the bank that set her coughing too. In the flash of an eye, she scooped me up and started running with me. Her otters were jumping on ahead, clearing a path for us. We passed between them, and they were lost from our sight among the trunks of the palm trees. All the while, Shathra was running from the white smoke and gasping for air.

She carried me into the water, and we reached a spot free of the smoke. I felt my lungs were on fire and could not stop coughing. That often happens to me when I inhale smoke. When I was eight, my father lit a cigarette and invited me to smoke it like he was. All the children in our church had been forced to do that by their fathers, who believed the rumor that smoking tobacco would protect us from the plague. My father was at the forefront of this belief. Fortunately, he was content to experiment only upon himself with the other remedies of warding off the plague, such as wrapping a dried frog around his finger, since he believed that using frogs as rings was protection against the Black Death.

Shathra wrapped her legs around me, and I submitted to the water's embrace. I floated along, curled over her shoulder, as she propelled me through the water, parallel to the bank. We ended up at a cucumber field, swarmed by a phalanx of rats that had fled the smoke, just like us. When I laid my head on the dirt, Shathra explained, in a compassionate tone this time, that the farmers would come across my leg. "They will plant it in the ground, and instead of one leg, you'll have seven!" I asked her to go back and get Baby Jesus and the Gospels before we continued on to the hospital. She helped me search for them for several minutes. Then, looking at the sun, she pulled me along. The hour was hanging in the heart of the gray sky. "We're late!" she cried. I didn't ask her to wait and search with me again. I submitted to the loss of my things. She had defeated me thoroughly, and she carried me over to her boat, which would take us back.

Even when we got into the boat and she began to row, she held me close to her body and prevented me from moving, using both her arms and her sharp odor of wet otters, which shocked the senses. She felt me squirming as I tried to reach my nose, and she eased her grip. I took a deep breath and scratched my nostrils. Then she began to talk. She had a heavy tongue that dragged out the consonants. They emerged heavily onto the tip of her tongue and then cast themselves, as though falling to their death, from her skillful mouth. She told me that the title of her profession—which no one was as good at as her—was "guide to the lost." In her biography—an oral history that I don't recommend anyone listen to—was a long list of names: all the children, travelers, and madmen she had rescued from their lost wanderings and brought back to their families, their guesthouses, and their hotels before sunset. I tapped at her ear from my position on her back, trying to get her to listen to me. She was carrying me with my back half dangling from her middle, as though I were a branch growing off her, without giving me room to get in a word edgewise. She kept going: "It's night now. You are the first lost person entrusted to me and my otters that I've brought back to their family after sunset."

I apologized and told her I was sorry. She sank into her own mind and was quiet for a long time. Then she tried to console me by saying it wasn't my fault. "The sun went down early today into the piggy bank. It's not our fault." She explained to me how there was someone who gathered suns under the earth and hoarded them in a piggy bank. He kept doing that with every sun that came each day, stuffing the sun at the end of that day into the bank so that the sunset could settle over all, gripping hearts, igniting sorrows, and provoking memories of departed loved ones.

Shathra sank into a long monologue, and her syllables found no difficulty in making their way through the air. A second important distinction of Shathra, who quickly became my friend, was that she was able to sense my invisible smile. It happened that, as we got nearer to the hospital, I smiled on the inside, only to feel her patting me on the back. I was delighted by what we saw—a large crowd of people whose lanterns stretched out in front of the hospital gate and to both sides. The crowd extended all the way to the harbor. The voices behind us were saying that Father Emmo had been found dead, floating face down as fish nibbled at his clothes and his blood.

I don't know why the talk of my father being killed and floating in the Shatt provoked a feeling of excitement. Perhaps it came from my obscure childish desire to be an orphan. Most of the girls I knew were orphans, or else had been abandoned by their fathers. Sometimes I lied and said my father had died so I would seem more like the others. I didn't like to be different. When I was corresponding with the children's magazine published by the Church of Latter-day Saints, they asked me for a short biography to put under my article. I exaggerated details about myself and concluded by saying, "and my father passed away two years ago." I never expected that same magazine to come into his hands. (I only placed it on his bed!) He did not get angry. He just bent his head toward my face until I could smell the soap he used for washing his hair. Then he danced with his eyes. He opened one while closing the other several times in a row as he said, "I'm alive! I'll die when you find a ladybug with eight spots." I was so ashamed that I cried from the pain of it. He squeezed my neck, which was the button he pressed in order to make me laugh. I felt him suck out all my feelings of shame and replace them with pure laughter.

Shathra adjusted her hold on my hip and walked forward with me. Disappointment mixed with relief when people said it was the body of a woman. As we approached Strangers Hospital, we neared the center of the crowd. My whole body was still pressed against Shathra, and there was no way for me to get away from her, so I merely asked her to do a kindness to my burning curiosity and take me inside the waves of people, crashing together around the floating story of a body. Shathra advanced. Everyone fell back and made a lane for us to pass, either out of reverence for Shathra or else in response to the blows on the neck she used to drive them away.

Before we were quite close enough to see the body, my face crashed into the ground when Shathra stopped suddenly, turned around, and lost her grip on me as she pulled me back in the direction of the hospital. The chattering people were passing around a description of the body: It was a water nymph, white as cotton. No conch covered her body; nothing covered her body. Various voices rose around me:

"Her fingers are more translucent than glass."

"And her nipples, like a pomegranate stem."

"She was laughing when she was killed . . ."

"How do you know? She doesn't have a head!"

"If she was laughing, it certainly wasn't from her mouth," said another, bursting out in wild laughter.

After the surprise died down and people stopped repeating the word *nymph*, they became more logical in their descriptions: "A naked woman, bare as the day God made her, with a bullet hole under her left breast." Whoever did it, according to the chatter of the people with their agitated syllables, had first slept with her and stripped off her clothes before killing her and throwing her in the Shatt so that she would be carried off by the currents. She would be lost in the branching veins of the river and find her way south, where she would be discovered by boatmen and fishermen, who would bring her to shore. Whoever did it had cut off her head and thrown it somewhere. On the topic of the nymph's head, Shathra had much to say, for she believed that heads that had been cut off sank to the bottom and then slowly floated back up some days later. This opinion of hers was enough to encourage the people's curiosity and keep them from rapidly moving on, just in case the head would float up that night.

The soldier who had stopped us before we reached the gate, who had a brown mustache that swayed like the pans of a scale, reached out a hand to Shathra and drew us under the leaning wall.

"Charlotte?" he said to me. "Yes, you are Charlotte. You have to come with me to the Chancery Office." That was his term for the wali's pen and its writer. I asked him where it was, and he replied, "The

Chancery Office is in the Qawnaq of the Wali Kadhim Pasha, khaton." That was the first time anyone had bestowed upon me the title of *khaton*, typically reserved for the noble ladies of the Turks and Mongols who ruled that city. The soldier uttered the name of the new Wali, Kadhim Pasha, deliberately and carefully so that it would exit his mouth correctly. Perhaps he feared his tongue would stumble on the names of the Ottoman walis, who hardly sat their bottoms on the throne before Istanbul exchanged them for a new one.

Shathra felt that her mission had ended. She released my hand and walked off toward the souk, looking deflated and despondent. At the time, I guessed it was because her glitter had been extinguished that night by the nymph, for normally, people would celebrate her, or at least reward her for leading their lost loved ones back. My hand, its pores momentarily able to breathe again, was suffocated once more by the gripping pressure of the soldier's hand. He picked me up and set me down on his elegant Hassawi donkey and led me down endless side streets filled with mules loaded with bags and with men—or with men who looked like bags—sleeping from the fatigue of the day. The longer the soldier's silence extended, the more frightened I became, until finally some of the few people walking there asked him about me, and why he was taking me with him, and how I had lost my leg. He didn't reply, just held my hand tightly, waving his other arm around my head to ward off the flies. I found myself in the Chancery Office. I expected my father would appear at any moment. Perhaps he had announced my loss and come there to get me back. But then, why hadn't Shathra taken me inside the hospital? That and other questions alternated in my mind. They were interrupted by the familiar voice of a man who came in the door. His hunchbacked shadow stretched across the floor ahead of him. He interlaced his hands behind his back. He smiled, and then he started chewing his lips as though to stop the flow of his emotions and keep his face frozen as he embraced me. It was my father's friend Davenport, a naval officer entrusted by the English to protect the American citizens in that area, including the small team at Strangers Hospital. I had seen him a few times on holidays and at evening parties, when my father allowed me to use the leg late into the night. He was a middle-aged man, and the gap between his eyebrows was adorned with red hair that shone in the light of the room. A floral scent preceded the heel strikes of his blue shoes. His operatic voice would call out names as though he were an announcer at a bullfight. He stepped back, freeing my chest from his embrace and falling on his knees in front of me. He said everyone was searching for me and that he was delighted at my safe return. As he spoke, he kept turning my hand over in his, examining it to make sure I was not injured, as though it were impossible for any other part of my body to be wounded. I do not know when he placed the towel on my face, but I suddenly felt a curtain shielding my view. He rubbed my head to dry it from the remains of the sweat that he thought were the traces of being so completely lost. I heard his voice through the curtain, meaning the towel that he had lowered over my face, even after he had stopped drying my head completely and his fingers came to rest. He continued speaking, telling me, "I heard that you've long wanted to see the place where the two rivers meet. Don't you know that no one is able to do that? It's because these two rivers don't actually meet. My friend, an engineer from Scotland named Ray, spent a quarter of a century here to study these rivers. One time, he drew for me his dangerous secret on the wall of his club in London. He drew the two rivers meeting, like they do on the map. Then he said they don't actually do that. The Tigris takes a certain amount of water from the Euphrates, and the Euphrates, diminished to that extent, continues on its way and gives birth to the river that you can see through that window. The One-Eyed Tigris acquired an undeserved reputation since it was not actually born in that meeting."

He could tell my attention was drifting, so he cleared his throat and added, "Shortly before you arrived, when word reached me that you had been carried back without your leg, I sent an announcement for the mule drivers to circulate news about a cash reward for whoever comes across your leg, a reward sufficient to make people rush to help us get it back. In the announcement, I mentioned that whoever finds it should give it to the guards at the hospital. Soon enough, you'll see and hear a happy surprise."

I bit my lower lip so that he might see I was paying attention to his words. Then, in a low voice, he said, "We might close the hospital tomorrow." He explained that such announcements had always produced an excessive result, and how, one time, he had announced in the *Al-Shati'* newspaper that an old tarboosh he had bought at the Tuesday market had gone missing. The next day, people brought him twenty tarbooshes in its place. I can't tell how he imagined this was any proof about the effectiveness of an announcement in the newspaper about my missing artificial leg, which might be the only one of its kind on the entire Arabian Peninsula. Nevertheless, my imagination offered me the picture of an endless line of men wearing tarbooshes stretching out from the door to my room, each one carrying a prosthetic leg inscribed with THIS IS THE LEG OF SOLDIER CORBIN O'HARO. THANK YOU.

I kept the question "Where's my father?" tucked under my tongue without asking it.

Davenport lifted the towel. A bead of sweat ran down from each of his temples onto his cheeks, which had been smooth before suddenly breaking into a smile and then turning into a frown. He began circling around the room of the wali's secretary, examining one of the photographs: an ostrich draped in gold and necklaces, being ridden by a bald girl and circling a square packed with a cheering crowd. He turned slowly and raised his eyes from the floor in a deliberate motion. "We haven't informed anyone that your father has not yet returned from his journey to search for you. Tomorrow afternoon, we'll send out seven boats to search for him. In my capacity as assistant deputy vice consul, I do not possess enough men to enable me to conduct an intrepid campaign to search for Father Emmanuel under every palm tree. But that doesn't mean that I won't actually try. It's necessary to communicate with the English consul, especially since the protection of all American lives here is entrusted to the British Crown."

He continued talking as he lifted me onto his hip and brought me back to Strangers Hospital and placed me on my bed himself. The commotion about the floating nymph was still going on everywhere, and because I was overstrained with the possibility of catching a cold, I contented myself with confirming the location of her body in the hospital so that I would know which window in my room looked out over her, where she lay shrouded in the great hall, since I was not permitted to open the back window, which looked out over a different part of the hall, because it was also pointed toward the mounds of trash from the Mohammedan fishermen. That was where they would throw the sharks, crabs, octopuses, and all the other sea creatures people didn't eat that ended up in their nets. Opening that window meant an abominable smell would invade us, mixing with the odor of decay rising from the lepers' isolation ward before it filled the entire upper floor.

I stayed up late, watching the nymph—the headless woman—asleep on the funerary table. A moonlit night, a window in an excellent corner, and a thread of sleepiness: it all helped me imagine the body of the nymph upon the gray covering. That was better than the crashing waves of people as they swarmed upon her. The sisters received her from the hands of the police after they had torn her away from the pouncing and kicking crowd. No one was certain of her humanity except the sisters at Strangers Hospital. The police had prepared her body and waited for the mosque imam, who would come twice a week to receive bodies and send them out to mosques and charnel houses to be washed and shrouded according to the religious rites of the Mohammedans. But this time was different. At first, they were not certain she was human, and the delay of her burial meant that her odor, which the water had suppressed, began circulating. The mosque imam refused to pray over her on the pretense that her identity, her religion, and her race were unknown. "The sea brings us everyone whose hand slips from the ship's railings," he said, "and it is not my duty to pray over everyone that has two legs."

We waited until the mufti put out a decree to settle the chaos. In it, he ruled that this woman was human: she had what women had and contained what they contained. As for her burial, he would like her to be buried in one of the foreigners' cemeteries. The sisters decided to bring the matter to Davenport, since they knew the assistant deputy vice consul was a friend of the hospital. He was even close at hand, ever since he had begun spending half his day in my father's room, keeping records of the tons of wool he was buying to export to New Jersey, as well as cleaning his fingernails and picking from the collar of his jacket all the goat hairs that were sticking there. With regard to the nymph, he decided to bury her in the cemetery founded by missionaries from the Protestant Evangelical Fathers. Perhaps he thought this eagerness to show kindness to everyone was an effective strategy to protect himself and his smuggling. So the nymph was carried by night to our cemetery, in which slept all the fathers of the mission who had been in charge of the task of preaching there before my father's time and before the construction of Strangers Hospital. The nurses prepared a grave marker in the name of Fatima, the name we bestowed upon the nymph. Actually, I was the one who suggested it, thinking *Fatima* was a better match than *Jane*, the name given to bodies of anonymous dead women in our own country.

SISTER BAGHDADLI AND WHAT GREW FROM HER

"True, its name is Strangers Hospital, but that does not mean that those who do not enter it are not strangers too," my father had said. "Just a few decades ago, three-quarters of the inhabitants of Basra died of the plague. Then the city was filled anew with other strangers. Whoever thinks you are a stranger is a stranger just like you—or at least, seventy-five percent of them are. In general, this term—*strangers*—is just a sign on a building or a mask that people wear. All of them are beloved by us and beloved by Christ. They hide behind the mask of stranger or outcast with no family and no doctor. All of them are our loved ones."

I remembered this discourse of my father's, which he proclaimed before me like a sermon. I recalled it in its entirety when I stared at strangers, both inside and outside the hospital, from the door of my room or from my balcony. *Perhaps I've actually begun to feel his loss,* I told myself.

Shathra stood behind the clay water cistern. A short fence of reed stalks that encircled the hospital separated her from me. She was utterly still; nothing moved but her eyelids, which closed and reopened in response to the pestering mosquitoes. It was as though that were her perpetual state whenever she announced her failure in searching for some lost person. She had informed us at dawn that she had found no trace of Father Emmo, and she did not believe she would be able to do anything in that regard, neither she nor her otters, which she carried with her in her pocket wherever she went—not the otters themselves, but rather, she signified each of them with a date pit, and she stashed the pits inside her clothes, giving a little bark at each one. So many times during the past few hours, I had seen her take the pile out of her pocket, spread them on the ground, and pick one of them up, place it inside her bosom, and then take another. One by one she would count them and then start all over with focused attention, as though she were running the accounts of a great cargo of goods.

"The mound of pits might grow or shrink, or her pocket might become completely empty," remarked Baghdadli, the second nurse at the hospital, who had been volunteering since the dawn prayers to serve as my leg until we found the missing artificial one. "Hello. I'm Sister Baghdadli, standing in for your leg, which is traveling to recuperate." That is how she had phrased it. Baghdadli, a Christian Arab who had converted from her Orthodox church to our church, had learned English in the north after enrolling in the Evangelical Protestant school there, where her family lived. They descended from the ancient Assyrian peoples, situated between two mountains, before she was expelled by her family and denied any food because she was corresponding with us—the American missionaries, that is. So she immigrated with our mission to Basra, renounced her status as a nun—indeed, as the former prioress of the Ephremite nuns. Alongside my father, she tried to interact with the Arabs, whose language she spoke better than all of us, perhaps, including the Arabs, in addition to her Assyrian language. Before my father arrived, she used to work with the mission in the north in the initial stages of its work there, which had begun aspirations to convert first the Christian Arabs to Protestantism, then the followers of Moses. Later on, they revised their aspirations and added the Mohammedans as a primary target. All that is to say that "my leg," in those days, spoke three languages, and she was a Christian from the north of the land of two rivers, taller than all the other nuns I had met. Quick to love and quick to cry, she was also direct and stubborn. She had just one defect—a tremor in all her limbs, like when a body is shook with epilepsy. If you approached her from behind, it was easy to startle her, and she was terrified anytime someone surprised her with their presence, especially at night. Oftentimes, I snuck up behind her and whispered her name. That would make her shudder and leap into the air, spouting the names of a dozen saints.

I was still studying Shathra as I leaned my head upon Baghdadli's hand. It was the right thing to do. I didn't resist playing that role. Even though I did not feel sad, it was not possible for me to show any feelings other than sorrow. Perhaps because I understood that sadness was what people expected of me, what I had to do, and what I had to submit to. People didn't give me any respite from the role of a girl who had lost her father when he went out searching for her.

And here, Shathra interrupted all employees of the hospital. She had been standing the whole day long behind the cistern, looking at me and gesturing whenever she noticed my head turning this way and that on the balcony. I watched her shadow stretch out behind her, trampled by the cows. She left that spot of hers and made her way toward the balcony. I don't know how she got past the guards at the gate. She lost her patience, abandoned her shadow, and came up. Sister Baghdadli smiled to see her approaching us. Shathra claimed that her stomach hurt, and she wanted a disinfectant salve to sterilize a wound in the hollow of her ear. She addressed me as "young doctor," apparently thinking that doctors gave birth to little doctors. Baghdadli put her fingers on Shathra's head and drew back her hair covering, which was stiff with blood. Shathra didn't show any gratitude. She reached out, grabbed me under the armpits, and brought me down from the chair where I was sitting. She carried me against her side, descending to the hall on the ground floor. When she noticed Baghdadli following us, she stopped and set me down on the tile floor. She apologized, said she would be on her way, and told Baghdadli not to be alarmed.

Two steps before reaching the middle of the staircase, Shathra dropped some object that had been hidden on her person. After falling from between her legs, a sticky fetus bounced down the stairs. Baghdadli, who was following close behind her, screamed and started babbling in Assyrian, turning in a full circle and making a prostration in each direction. That falling part of Shathra kept rolling down the stairs until it came to rest on the floor below. Shathra was content with giving it a passing glance before she left us and disappeared out the door. Baghdadli rushed to the kitchen to retrieve a fork, which she used to turn the fetus over. I closely followed her actions, and she gave me a look that said it was not appropriate for teenagers to witness such things. All the while, the puddle of blood beneath us was spreading.

Baghdadli's mouth split in a slowly liberated smile. I did not understand what was happening until the fork plunged deep into that fetus and confirmed for me, as well as for her, that it was only a globular fish, smooth, without a shell. Several seconds passed, and then Shathra stuck her head through the window of the red door. Actually, the sound of her exploding into laughter came first. Shathra clapped and sat down on the bench. Baghdadli said that she had done that before to frighten her or to provoke her disgust. But she prayed in the names of the saints each time Shathra provoked her, whenever she took a fish of that kind and threw it at her—or birthed it in her direction. Shathra's jokes were rare, but when they happened, they shattered all the affection and any modicum of respect she'd had previously. Perhaps it was useful, for that joke allowed me to interact with her in my own way without holding fast to my father's teachings about speaking with the Arabs around the harbor. And it actually was the case that my relationship with Shathra changed entirely after that joke of hers. Perhaps that was her intention.

Our three-person sessions—Shathra, Baghdadli, and me—continued on dozens of occasions over the days that followed the disappearance of my father. The two of them spent time with me to console me.

And I projected a feigned desire for my father that persuaded them that I was upset. I would sing, they would read to me, and I would read to them from my articles—that is to say, the broken wings of my articles. I received Baghdadli's gifts and the strange dishes she cooked, which went beyond bread, and I can truly say that the offerings of bread she made were the most delicious things to have ever passed my lips. I can still taste that salty flavor between my molars despite the long decades that have passed since the last time I saw Baghdadli and her bread.

A day or two after my return to the hospital, Baghdadli placed a necklace around my neck. It was a string woven from palm leaves, from which hung a piece of brass: a bullet with one end removed and hollowed out, leaving enough space for a rolled-up piece of paper. She said she removed that very bullet from the water nymph's chest. In that country, bullets used in a murder were taken apart to search for secret papers contained inside, since it happened that killers often put some kind of message into their bullets by cramming the paper inside the hollow space. Usually, doctors or those who washed the dead were the first to read those messages before they found their way to the trash can. The bullet from Fatima, formerly known as the nymph, was empty. It contained nothing written inside, even though the bullet and its hollow were big enough to contain a novel.

That evening, Davenport visited, and we formed a circle around him. He gave an account of the teams he had sent to search for my father. There was nothing serious or clear to report yet. He finished his words by stating his intention to take us with him the next day, for it had reached his well-paying ears that the death row at the prison of the Qawnaq contained a man who resembled my father. In that country, those who were about to have their heads cut off were placed in a dim outer room at the far end of the Qawnaq—the wali's palace—in view of soldiers distributed upon the four surrounding towers. According to Davenport's spies and the eyes he had planted in this city like mushrooms, there was a white man with a shaved face who looked like my father and was awaiting his final day in captivity. Davenport thought the Turks were holding Dr. Emmanuel prisoner and that they would write his final chapter, along with other men condemned to die on various charges, without announcing his identity, letting his head be lost among the other heads rolling on the shore. When he pondered it further, just a little bit further, he decided to speak with the wali himself. All it would take for the governor to resolve the wool merchant's doubts was the certainty of an eyewitness, which needed no debates, motions, or verbal quarrels. They set a time for the people of the missing Emmanuel to visit the prison and make sure for themselves about the spurious charge.

Shathra was our guide to the address written on the back of the hand of the assistant deputy vice consul. We rode for approximately twenty minutes and dismounted at a distance of just a few meters from the wali's Qawnaq, behind which was said to be the execution chamber. Shathra led the way around the governor's fort, though we did not manage to emerge from the labyrinth drawn by our steps. The Qawnaq resembled a military barracks. It was surrounded by small towers, where we could see soldiers perching, though Shathra said they were only wooden human statues. After I became certain we were lost, I called out to her and tugged on her braid, which emerged from under her head covering and hung down her back. I asked her to do something, but she was obstinate as a mule. More unmoving than stone, she stubbornly refused to ask about the road from the passersby so that we might find our way out of that maze. Davenport backed her up, pleading the excuse that it was dangerous to communicate with the people, especially to reveal one's ignorance and ask for help.

Shathra was perplexed, and she made her way sluggishly. What increased her sense of confusion is that children from the market were following us, barking and pelting us with the seeds of rotten watermelons. They imitated the sounds of dogs in all their various states: a dog barking as it attacks, a dog whining as though run over by a cart, and yet another making the sound of a dog fawning over its master. The number of them seemed to be increasing until it became our primary concern to get back to the hospital in one piece. We gave up entirely the matter of the prison, and when the troop of barking boys was out of sight, Shathra led us down alleys so narrow she had to walk crabwise, with me sitting on her shoulders. As soon as we emerged, we were confronted by boys from the next neighborhood over. They all started barking and chasing after Shathra's abaya so that one of them would step on it and we would fall on our faces. But that didn't happen, for a licorice-stick vendor chased the boys away by spraying them with dirty water. We resigned ourselves to walking back along the river, and he said goodbye to us, laughing, after having given a bark of his own as he patted Shathra's back. At that, we were certain it was no laughing matter to accompany Shathra, as we might have assumed. I held back my question about why the people around her had been barking until we were all in a better mood.

On the second attempt, one of the hospital guards accompanied us to the address. Before we reached the wooden bridge leading to the prison and the execution chamber, Shathra became agitated and started shaking. She slapped her thigh and said, "The prison is over here. Right over here!" Davenport laughed at her and asked how she could know that this time. She made him uncomfortable with how close she got to him to give her long reply, breathing into his ear as she spoke. The essence of her response was that, in contrast to her talents with people, she was not an expert at finding houses because she could not distinguish between the colors of the doors. Words like *red* and *green* always confused her since she did not perceive what they referred to. Lost people, on the other hand, had familiar colors: various shades of brown, black, and sometimes even white. She had hidden that truth to conceal her weakness, and she described her anxiety at the boys chasing her with their ear-piercing barks.

The wali, who had perhaps reached his ninth decade, was sitting cross-legged in the corner. He gripped his beard—which was dyed with henna on its conical lower half, leaving the upper half white—indifferent to the striking resemblance between his face and a banana dipped in date syrup. He had decided to bring us to his residence rather than the prison and to summon the prisoner to kneel at his feet. We arranged ourselves there, facing his throne and with our backs against curtains decorated with gazelles running through sycamore trees. When the prisoner was brought in, they made room for him off to the side, and where he stood, a somber gazelle peeked out from behind his veiled head. Three soldiers from the Qawnaq were there, lined up on the side opposite him, where there were no gazelles. The wali began speaking, striking his chest as he did so, explaining his good intentions and his excessive interest in caring for foreigners. He recalled the sociable moments and the charming nights that he had convened with the assistant deputy vice consul, while the latter followed the sinuous branches in the carpet with his eyes. The wali emptied his crop of all its amicable words, dousing the room entirely with gestures of respect, flattery, and brotherhood. Davenport broke into performance to praise the wali's kind words even as he hinted that he still was not completely convinced. The wali bid the soldiers to raise the veil from the face of the prisoner.

From the moment he entered, I was certain that this man was not my father. Baghdadli took a long breath when she saw the proof in the man's face. It was a young man with fair skin and not the least bit of resemblance to my father. Perhaps the color of his hair and skin had muddled the minds of the Arabs and Turks there, and some of them who love inventing tall tales had dreamed up this nonsense of a likeness.

Davenport exchanged looks with the wali, who ordered the prisoner to be brought back to his room. The young man began screaming, but the sound was drowned out by the booming call to prayer, which came to us from behind the curtains as they started dragging him away in front of our eyes. The volume diminished and then rose again as they pushed him along and he crashed into something. The man cursed the guards, who converged upon him, knocking him flat on his chest and laying into him with their whips.

◆ ◆ ◆

I informed Davenport that I would take Shathra to live with me for the rest of my time in that city. He refused on the pretense that the lady was not immunized against leprosy and smallpox. When he saw my face breaking as I struggled to make a weak, disjointed response, he promised without my asking to undertake the task of immunizing and disinfecting her. It happened that Shathra moved in and lived, for the most part, on my balcony. Some of the vendors who roamed the city caught sight of her through the openings in the balustrade, crawling among the plaster flowers that decorated the balcony. When their eyes fell upon her, up rose the barking, but it began to lose its effects, on both me and her. It no longer bothered us, and I didn't take it upon myself to ask what it meant. It even happened that the barking died away in the streets, where we walked in Baghdadli's company. When we went out walking, no one pursued us any longer. I would wrap myself around the waist of one of them while my right foot dragged along the ground, drawing an invisible line that said nothing, and we would reach our destination safely.

Sometimes when we went out, Shathra would take pleasure by playing in the mud, as though digging a trench to reinforce the hospital fence. She sang a little and swayed her head. Then she told me a number of disjointed, unrelated stories. I don't know—maybe she was just singing and some of the songs had no melody. They came out of her like memorized prayers she was reciting without any rhyme or reason, just a nervous twitch of her tongue, as though she was used to repeating them at length in front of some audience. She told me of her father in the village of Umm al-Jurukh in the lakes region, surrounded by the folds of the vast green marsh, up there where the two rivers meet. He was famous for his noble profession of pulling teeth and performing castrations and circumcisions. Her mother had died after giving birth to Shathra's twin sisters. They had cost Shathra so much effort that people considered her their mother, a role she imitated and sometimes even claimed. Their father would disappear for weeks and return with sweets, clothes, and the eggs of ducks and moorhens, which he would place in the corner of the reed room that was reinforced by a ring of glass bottles. With the proceeds from weeks of toil, he would roam off to the city to buy perfume and spoons and shawls embroidered with threads of silk and fake gold. He would return with all that under his coat of thick fur, which he never took off, not even when the sun blazed down, for without it, no one would hire him to pull out their teeth or entrust him to circumcise children and castrate slaves. Due to the demands of his trade and how long he had been at it, the girls' father acquired prodigious skills and became the life of a social gathering, seasoning the long winter nights as much as people season their food with salt. He developed the ability to tell stories, jokes, and the supernatural feats of the jinn. That last was the easiest part of his genius, for as he saw it, the jinn do everything and transform into everything, so the task of concocting a story with one of the jinn as its hero took no effort at all. He would improvise according to his need whenever he wanted to pacify a patient's sense and grant a sense of calm. It would not reduce the nightmarish pain in the patient's mouth, but it granted a brief moment of distraction. The stories would numb him, his head filled with their poison, and the metal forceps would seize the opportunity to rip out whatever seemed necessary, be it a tooth or the foreskin of a penis.

For the daughter of Sheikh Hadrallah, the leader of Umm al-Jurukh, these stories of Shathra's father did not enter her ears casually, but with the kind of passion that can split a villager's head from the intensity of love songs that throb with desire. As Shathra described it to me, it is necessary to bind the hearts of the girls in the village with ties and chains to keep them from falling in love. Despite all that, this girl was drawn to the man's voice before she even saw him. She continued to learn of his activities from the mouths of all her cousins, and it was only a few weeks before the marks of love appeared on the face of Shathra's father. Yearning for the sheikh's daughter lit up his forehead like a lighthouse. Not only his face betrayed him but his words as well. He even began to call his daughters by their names. Even so, Shathra thought it likely that the sheikh's daughter loved her father more than he loved her. A scandal arose after the passionate woman allowed her belly the freedom to swell, and she became pregnant by the older man. Perhaps she had been determined to reveal her story through the rumors that reached everyone's ears. These stories provoked the girl's cousins, who refused the request of Shathra's father to make an offer of marriage to their kinswoman. They could not stomach the idea that they would be related by marriage to a tooth-extractor with a bevy of batty daughters. They sent him a warning. At that, he released the reins of his anger, despite his certainty that no one would be able to contend with the authority of Sheikh Hadrallah in the village of Umm al-Jurukh. The situation ended badly for Shathra's father: bound hand and foot, ribs shattered, sprawled on his face in the presence of all the men and boys of the village—and under the eyes of the women who stole glances through gaps in the reed walls. It was a tribal court, the kind of event that leaves an indelible impression on the memory of anyone who witnesses one during their childhood. Shathra was in her second decade at that time. She left her two younger sisters in their room and found a place where she could eavesdrop on the proceedings and catch the decision of the judges. The sentence they passed upon him was to grant his two daughters to the two sons of Sheikh Hadrallah as atonement for his deed. Haste was made to carry out the judgment quickly. The sheikh climbed onto the back of Shathra's father and heard his ribs crunch as he ground them under his feet. Yet the sheikh's rage burned still brighter, and he felt the need to let it breathe. He puffed out a wave of hot air from his nose. He struck his chest and his forehead in regret and anger. He screamed in the faces of the judges that their sentence would not extinguish his vengeance, and it would never restore to his house its dignity or his daughter, who was murdered by her brothers to preserve the family's honor in the face of such a scandal—his own daughter, whose flesh the worm would never dare to gnaw under the ground, on account of her extreme virtue and honor, along with the intensity of her splendor and courage, her skill at doing everything, from riding horses to riding the backs of her enemies. He addressed them, reminding them of his honor, his virtues, and his superiority over them all. While he was unsheathing his most eloquent expressions and his most persuasive epithets, the barking of a dog interrupted him. It was the sheikh's dog, named Hosrim Pasha, a name chosen to proclaim to every visitor that this village called their dogs by the names of walis and officials of the Turks, and that they were not afraid of anyone. Hosrim Pasha entered the very heart of the majlis, gazing about at the people as though he were a venerable leader, and then plopped down at the feet of the sheikh, who kicked him in the head to move him away a few paces. The dog swung its head back and forth from the pain while the sheikh returned to the far end of the spacious hall of reeds, feeling regret for having harmed the tribe's dog. Hadrallah cried aloud to the judges, "Let him die! And his daughters go to my sons, the elder and the younger. As for his insane daughter, we'll take her too and marry her to the dog." The judges of the lakes had never before decreed to marry a girl to a dog. The matter struck the audience like a stone, a silence falling among the assembly. It was followed by another silencing stone as the sheikh went on to say, "Not to this dog of mine, but to the water dog!" A common Arabic name for *otter*. The people carried out those judgments that very day.

Shathra slept that night in a room without a roof, together with a dozen otters, not knowing which among them was her husband. She kept expecting to hear the sobs of her sisters when the men performed their virility upon them, for night in Umm al-Jurukh concealed no sounds. The murmuring talk of people outside their rooms and diwans amounted to a general proclamation to passersby and also to her, but the night closed its revelations before reaching its middle hour. It let down its black curtain, and the company of her new amphibious family was calmer than she had expected.

◆ ◆ ◆

Baghdadli did not prevent my coming along to the public executions that occurred along the shore. Executions had become the custom with the appointment of every new wali, and they did not produce anything beyond boredom in people's hearts. All curiosity had been snuffed out on account of the gruesome methods of executing hyenas to terrify the lions that the walis assiduously pursued. Each new wali hastened to gather a handful of robbers, criminals, merchants using dishonest scales, and other various misfortunates. He would throw some of them in prison and execute others. The clamor of the city would die down, and they would not cease to be scourged by plagues and by gangs of sheikhs and princes all over again, at least until the wali was exchanged for someone new. The walis were always being exchanged, and their reign would never last for three years. Kadhim Pasha was a man of that soil and that era, and it was as though Davenport had him by the balls: the wali refused none of Davenport's demands, and the only demand he made in return was that Davenport be satisfied. According to Sister Baghdadli, who wormed her way among the people and sniffed out every story, Kadhim Pasha—carrying the rank of silahdar from Istanbul, a leader of armies—had come to stay, so it was to his advantage to please all the well-to-do in that city, as well as the not so well-to-do.

We were in the hospital pharmacy when Baghdadli commented that the wali had come for rest and relaxation, and that he would perform executions as though he were picking his teeth. She also told me that Davenport's brain was bent on trade and making a profit. He closed some mouths here and opened others there, and sooner or later they would arrive at a satisfactory bargain in some domain, be it wool or oil or women. Perhaps she was trying to say she had experience with people and knew their nature from her dealings with them in the past, and especially with Davenport. At the time, I chalked it up to the clear tension between those two individuals whenever they met. She did not respond to his flattery, nor did she have much to say in his presence, even though he never gave up trying to communicate with her. The best example of that is what happened when we met him at the scene of the execution, to which he had no doubt been invited and did not have to find a place to steal a view, as did Baghdadli and I.

Those executions were not the first attempts by Kadhim Pasha to send the ghost of fear among the people. In his first week, he plucked some men from prison and ordered the jailers to help his soldiers squeeze them into rice sacks. The sacks were tied shut and attached with ropes to the pillars supporting the bridge. They let the water toss the corpses around for six days as an admonition to those who might take warning—and those who wouldn't. And also to the curious who murmured observations about the color of the Shatt when we soaked six prisoners in it whose faces had not felt the sun's heat for months. But apparently, he considered that people's memories are written in hookah smoke; periodically, they needed to be refreshed.

As for me, what drew me that day was a close observation for a second time of the man falsely said to resemble my father. Before that, I had stood at the heads of corpses and even half—nay, quarter—corpses in the halls of my father or during journeys along the road when we saw the remnants of caravans after brigands had fallen upon them. But I was unable to learn the charge leading this man to his death. Indeed, no success came to any of our troop of disappointed people, made up of a nun who had recently changed her sect, a guide for the wandering lost, and me.

Under the blazing sun, the wali gathered with a line of soldiers, their horses and mules standing behind them. The executioner led a middle-aged man down to the bank. His bones nearly crumbled beneath him, the way a dead tree might collapse. Baghdadli, Shathra, and I were watching from afar. I felt Baghdadli meow with disgust when Davenport approached us. He smiled, but the rest of the features of his face were saying, "You shouldn't be here." Thereafter, he appointed himself interpreter and translator for what happened among the wali's retinue and in the execution. Perhaps the change in the weather that day contributed to a sudden lessening of my enthusiasm, and were it not for Baghdadli's vivacity, I would undoubtedly have fallen asleep on my feet. No matter what Davenport said, she responded with some meaningless sound, either a long *mm-hmm* or a faint but regular *haaa* that lasted until her lungs ran out of oxygen. Then she tried the voices of wolves, squirrels, and crickets. That did not seem to have any effect on his commitment to exhausting himself in service to us that day.

Davenport informed us that after the execution, the wali would announce a reward for whoever found Dr. Emmanuel. He had chosen that occasion in order to guarantee a large crowd of people, which would broaden the reach of the announcement. That way, the news would not be lost among the barefooted men of the assembly, for everyone was interested to know the fate of this middle-aged man with sagging limbs. At that point, Baghdadli cut him off, speaking first in Arabic to put a halt to his discourse. Then she continued in English, completing the words he had begun and adding, "This man's charge is claiming divinity. His issue has reached the four corners of the city, after witnesses heard him making that claim. When he gathered a flock of adherents around him, people complained to the judges, who published a paper from the mufti containing permission for punishment."

The sun disappeared for some minutes behind a yellow cloud. A general moment of silence presided, followed by a sound from the man claiming divinity as he coughed. The disinterested brick-carriers chattered as they passed by, saying, "They are going to execute God." The man's eyes were hollow, and he was breathing with difficulty. He focused on tightening his belt so that his pants would not fall down and expose his privates to the people, for it had already happened that when the executioner was pulling him by his vest, he stepped on the hem of the man's trousers, which had fallen down and revealed his underwear. We heard what the people were saying in the crowds on the other side of the Shatt. Even though it would not have been easy for them to see the privates, or something just as bad in their reckoning, they still made a joke about the appearance of the Lord's privates, which the condemned man turned to hear. He smiled as though what he were undergoing were nothing more than an ordinary embarrassing situation. Then he went pale again in front of the executioner, who gave him only the briefest respite before forcing him to his knees and sweeping his head off his body. The head rolled down the sloping bank. It smacked against the shell of a dead turtle on its determined path toward the Shatt. After that, the scene of the execution of my father's doppelgänger contained nothing to hold our interest. According to expectations, it began and finished quickly, even before the laws of physics finished their task of rolling into the river the head of the man who'd claimed divinity.

I noticed that the letters of the word STRANGERS on the hospital sign had become fouled with bird droppings that had dried upon it like frozen tears. I entered with Baghdadli, pretending to ignore Davenport where he lay sprawled in a bed on his face. In the morning, I wheeled out a cart and climbed upon it to clean the sign by scrubbing it with soap. I saw that Davenport had not left, but had just carried himself to a different bed, unconcerned about the shapes his contorted body made, nor about the stains from his sweat that had turned the sheets into maps. He slept so deep that he paid no heed to the pile of journals and folded clothes underneath his head, pressed down by his cheek and soiled with a thread of his spittle. I went back to him once I was finished cleaning the droppings off. After pulling the pile of magazines out from under him, I put back the Arabic journals *Al-Muqtataf* and *Al-Hilal* and the newspaper *Al-Zawra'*. But I grabbed one thick journal: the new edition of the *Tigris-Euphrates Valley Mission*. It was the issue with my most recent article, and I had been waiting impatiently for it to arrive. Davenport's drool had soaked into my picture, a photograph I had taken in my twelfth year on this earth. It appeared above my article, which I had sent them seven months earlier. In their infinite wisdom, however, they had taken it upon themselves to change its title from "How Did Sargon of Akkad Appear with Red Lips?" to "My Visit to Sargon's Palace in Babylon and His Story in the Book of Exodus." I turned my eyes away from the text of the article. I did not like to read my words after they were offered up to readers, whom I felt were treating me harshly. There was something I liked very much about being published, without a doubt, but I did not like the feeling that people were reading what I wrote. It was like they were removing my clothing, one item at a time, until I was left stark naked. There was another reason behind my aversion, which is that my articles were published in the children's section, alongside hymns and the most foolish, juvenile stories sent in by the children of missionaries, but which most likely were written by their parents. It was awful! What I remember of that article was that I recounted the story of Sargon and how, after his mother placed him in the water inside a basket, the waves took him to the home of the king. I was fascinated by that story. Something about it captured my imagination and made me wish my own birth had a similarly exciting story. I could never be comfortable with the idea that my childhood was ordinary. Under the article was a lengthy letter sent by Madelena, the second of the nuns who worked as supernumerary nurses at Strangers Hospital. In it, she described her ability to care for more than forty Arab women in a single day. She mentioned that she would give them a consultation card containing everything the doctor needed in order to review the history of the condition and the medicine that had been prescribed. On the other side of the card was a drawing of Christ. One time, a middle-aged woman who was suffering from conjunctivitis came, her baby on her shoulder. Once she had been treated, the nurse asked permission to examine the bruise under her eye. After she rubbed it and sterilized it, the woman asked Madelena to exchange the card with another that did not have a picture of that man—meaning Christ—on the back side. With some difficulty, the nurse was able to comply with the request. When she inquired as to the reason, the woman said her husband struck her in the face and swelled her eye shut after seeing the consultation card, with its image of some strange man, in her closet.

The rest of the articles were the usual sort found in every issue: a brief note from the editor in chief, who was spending his holiday in Rome; a photograph of patients in their beds, with an explanation of their illnesses; a detailed report by a newly commissioned missionary, who recounted the foods and beverages he had consumed on his journey. In the final pages, there were brief reports about the transfers of priests, nuns, and doctors from Arab countries to America, the names of the ships conveying them, and the dates of embarking and docking. As usual, there was not much that excited me in the pages of journeys or the well-wishes for arrivals and departures—not until my own name jumped out at me, which my eye always spotted at once, as though it called out to me. Ever since the first time my name was published in the journal, along with a picture of me being held by my father, my name often appeared as a journal correspondent who published her objections and criticisms in the correspondents' column. Then I began to write to them periodically, and I asked my father to write to the journal, in his own name and address, to ask them to stop publishing the picture of us together every time I wrote an article. It was a picture of me sitting in front of him, with my artificial leg stretched out before us. That was all it took to drown me in letters in the month that followed, a raft of compassionate words that made me feel sick, which made my hair fall out and my tongue dry out. We exchanged it for another photo, something older but more appropriate and prettier.

I grabbed the journal and dragged myself to my room in order to savor the paragraph focused on me: "The steamship *Atlantis* embarked one morning last May, carrying Emmanuel, the esteemed priest and magnanimous doctor, in the company of his learned daughter, that princess of puzzles and peculiar tales, a storyteller as promising as she is preeminent, Charlotte Emmanuel. Returning to Seattle, they arrived last Saturday evening at the North Harbor, accompanied by the Lord's pleasure and preserved in His blessed care."

That date corresponded with none other than last week. I felt a mild dizziness and lost my balance. Suddenly, I was delighted to feel like I was stepping inside a detective story written by Sir Arthur Conan Doyle. The whole thing seemed as frightening as it was thrilling, and it made me think about the indigo butterfly that had come to rest upon the nose of the assistant deputy vice consul.

I did not wake Davenport up. I put the folded journal into my pocket and called for Baghdadli. I thought that Davenport was about to get rid of me. By announcing the return of my father and me to America, he had planted the idea in everyone's mind that we were no longer present in Basra. Everything that would happen to me was now an unwritten life, unacknowledged in the archives. In other words, nonexistent: a period of time that slipped out of the back pocket of history, present in some almanac in the mind of my father or in the mind of Davenport. But it was not my time.

If you have the opportunity to come across every issue of that journal, the *Tigris-Euphrates Valley Mission*, with all its news of the missionaries volunteering to preach the Gospel overseas and all the encyclopedic details about the lives of the families of the missionaries and their day-to-day affairs, you will read about the day we left, my father and I. Indeed, you will even find some articles about our life in Seattle. A dozen photos. Correspondence and written records about our life after my father's retirement from his passion for preaching and his subsequent leisure devoted to raising pigs on the shores of Lake Washington. But if you trust me, you will know that none of that ever happened.

THE SECOND QUARTER

TIGERS IN STRANGERS HOSPITAL

The head of the water nymph had still not floated to the surface. The One-Eyed Tigris still did not spit it out. "Why do I have to believe Shathra's physics and deny the physics of our church?" I asked myself as I abandoned my habit of standing along the Shatt, waiting for the nymph's head.

Most people called the reward that Kadhim Pasha had promised for whoever came across my father "The Old Man's Reward," referring to the person who offered it, whose age approached a full century. Some people, however, called it "Father Emmo's Reward" or "The Englishman's Reward," referring to my father, because most people considered us to be English—with the exception of Shathra, who believed us to be Turks because we used a new type of soap.

The third day passed listlessly without any news or indications to speak of, with the exception of one thing. We did not consider it anything official because it was supported by the flimsiest of rumors. But even if it wasn't an expectation that my father would suddenly show up at the door, it was an indication of a hope we could watch out for—something preferable by far to insisting that Davenport speed up his search. It happened when I finally met Rahlo. I had heard her name repeated time and again in all corners of the hospital, as well as in its records and schedules. She was the mistress of a house of prostitutes at the head of the river, where a light was constantly lit above bowers made from the trunks of palm trees and fig trees stuck together. From there the singing voices of men could be heard, accompanied by music played with plates, spoons, and pitchers. Rahlo was its proud director, and her reputation preceded her everywhere. She enjoyed the protection of gangs of retired fishermen and old men who used to work the sea, none of them younger than sixty. They needed only their voices and their words to maintain the security of the house and preserve the flow of its necessary services. The names of the prostitutes, as well as their sexual organs, were well known, given how often men used them to make their oaths, vows, and promises. I once heard a man, present at the hospital with a patient whose ear had been torn off, swear by the breasts of some woman that the girl had cut off her own ear, and it was likely that those breasts in the vow belonged to one of the favorite prostitutes whose bodies he could admire but not penetrate on account of his advancing years. Sister Baghdadli had translated what the man said, her eyebrows shooting up to show she did not believe him. Such oaths held no weight with us, and we paid no attention to its translation, not needing it in the first place.

Rahlo, who was almost Baghdadli's best friend, was a woman in her late fifties. Her most prominent feature was the lines on her palm, which were as defined as the borders of the various kingdoms on the map. It was as though some scrivener had decorated her palm with notches. As for her blindness, I would repeatedly see that her useless eyes suggested the opposite, pointing forward and shining despite being extinguished. My father had come across blind prostitutes numerous times during his mission to preach the gospel of the kingdom of heaven in those parts. As he explained it to me, the mud of the river is transformed and turns to dry land in a certain season of the year, and it brings with it a pitch-black darkness that snatches the eyes if it touches the faces of children bathing in the river. In that way, a child emerges from the river clean but blind. The blind grow up, both female and male, and dedicate themselves to memorizing the Qur'an. They often have gifted, melodic voices that enchant the listener with their intonation of the words. Their recitations of the Qur'an guarantee them a living and freedom from a life of wandering the roads to beg. In the case of Rahlo, her steps took her down a different path. Even her voice, which she lubricated with ginger and sang every day, screeched like a door made of ivory.

"My name is Rahayla, but it changed to Rahlo," she said. "People here add an *o* to the end of names: the *o* of the sea."

I do not deny that her friendship with Baghdadli was yet one more trait among many that were as startling as the etched lines of her palm. It will be obvious that the companionship of a nun and a prostitute was not a traditional arrangement, but perhaps that was in keeping with Baghdadli's general spirit when interacting with people, especially the aversion that ran contrary and made her not resemble her peers, especially the other sister who, like her, helped my father in the hospital.

We did not come into each other's proximity before the night of the carnival. At midnight, there was a knock at my door. I opened to find Baghdadli standing there. She asked if she could help me get dressed, and I proceeded to put on my best clothes and braid my hair. I didn't ask where we were going until she draped my body in a Mohammedan abaya. She put one on, too, cut to her own size, though hers was short and scarcely reached her knees. When she walked, Baghdadli swaggered like a sultaness. Her long spine remained erect, even when she jumped over a small irrigation ditch. With an abaya that revealed half her full dress, her appearance was the very thing to arouse curiosity and stick in people's minds. We went to a shop for mirrors. The shopkeepers dusted off their goods and displayed them on both sides of the door. By the full moon and the lights coming from the harbor, I was able to see what we looked like, Baghdadli and I. It only took one look at me, sprouting from the side of a towering Arab lady, to make all the mirror vendors turn toward us, their mouths hanging open. I couldn't blame them. It's not every day that a man sees a girl with one leg growing off the hip of a nun disguised in a Mohammedan abaya.

It was not far to our destination. Before long, I could see she was taking me to a marriage procession, lit by lights shining far into the night and only a few meters from the execution of my father's doppelgänger who claimed divinity. A crowd of people carried candles, lanterns, banners, and drums. Wearing green hats embellished with colorful and elaborate decorations, they encircled a young girl in white clothes. They carried small staffs and played with them like swords. Some cradled their sticks as though they were rifles, loading them and aiming them. Behind them was a line of slaves playing the flute and beating small drums made from clay and goatskins. Last of all was a team of mute violin players, shaking their heads as they played and looking as though they did not even hear their instruments.

It seemed that Baghdadli had devoted herself to this activity often, disguising herself in Mohammedan garb and slipping out to her own cave of secrets and losing herself among those women. This time it was a joyous celebration, wrapped in noisy excitement, singing, and children dancing. Baghdadli made me understand that the occasion for this gathering was a celebration for the arrival of a ship carrying some of the Prophet Mohammed's hair. An announcement had circulated from the diwan of Kadhim Pasha that some hairs from the Prophet Mohammed were voyaging across the sea in chests gilded with silver and gold and lined with silk, making their way through that realm to Istanbul, where the chests would be opened in the presence of the august sultan. Having originally set out from the Hejaz, the ship would pass the night on the One-Eyed Tigris after having completed a long tour through Bombay and Sumatra.

Baghdadli whispered to me that she would draw Rahlo into our coterie so that we could enjoy the carnival together. She gestured toward where Rahlo stood among the brightest of her followers, watching what went on. Like everyone else, she was waiting to catch a glimpse of the ship as it passed northward. One of her companions noticed us and walked her in our direction. I had expected that meeting Rahlo would mean an audience with a half-naked woman dressed in scandalous, revealing clothes, with decorations and the scars of stabs, burns, and ancient wounds, along with other reminders left behind on her body by the drunkards of the shore. Instead, I beheld a woman who made me feel like an adolescent girl. My head hung with shame. I had entered that city inside a bottle that protected me from the likes of her. Without intending to, my father had drawn a curtain that shielded me from all his patients who resembled Rahlo, a woman who disappointed your wicked thoughts and tamed both your expectations and your naive intuitions.

When we were close enough for her to hear our voices, she hurried forward to offer her greetings. She had veiled her face and was even cautious of showing her toes under her abaya. Perhaps the mild breezes of the night, like me, did not believe in the reality of the image that Rahlo presented, for the wind, mixed with smoke from the Indians' kitchens, played with her form, pulling away the covering from various parts of her body. That is what made me pass my eyes over the men who gathered around us, dumbstruck. They were frozen in place, and nothing twitched or pulsed except the pupils of their eyes, which danced with confusion, following the way the air and the faint light played upon the folds of clothing around Rahlo's trunk and the proud fruit of her chest. From both her words and the familiar way she snapped at Shathra, I knew that Shathra had rented a small bower in the large brothel that Rahlo managed with efficient expertise. Baghdadli laughed as she told me that Rahlo had absorbed the arts of leadership from the naval officers who visited her house in the nighttime. When she heard the police were on their way, she had her girls alter the features of the building in just a few minutes so that the police entered a chaste residence that raised no suspicions and gave the lie to the informers. But that situation did not last long. The matter usually ended with a bribe paid to the police officer, who would doff his cap and humbly sit on the ground, and Rahlo's men would place a small amount of money inside it. The officer would count the coins, go away, and then come back after a week, threatening to drag everyone off to the police station.

Rahlo, the blind prostitute, spoke Arabic without the letter *r*, on account of a defect in her tongue, even though it was the only language she knew apart from some greetings in English and Portuguese that various captains had slipped into her ears. I'm not counting her body language, which the men on the boats understood very well after they'd been drawn in by her widespread reputation.

The ship passed by, the great lanterns hanging on both sides swinging with the motion of the waves. The flags fluttering with the sails, windows draped with red velvet, men in white turbans preceded by their perfume and their smiles—it all drove the execution ceremony from my memory. I noticed the whole group—Shathra, Baghdadli, and Rahlo—smiling and breathing deep the air of that scene. I cannot deny that Rahlo's laughter erased any suspicions we had that the water nymph was connected to her. Her face would never have been able to relax like that if the fish had been nibbling the corpse of one of her girls just days before.

The people dispersed when soldiers fired three warning shots to scatter the crowd. We hurried along again, all except Baghdadli, who fell face down on the ground as soon as she started moving. We picked her up, and she clapped us on the back of the neck. Rahlo stuck with us that night, and we entered Strangers Hospital together. "I want to see the water nymph," she said. She did not believe that anyone would bury the body, because its mystique and beauty would not decay. We had heard the same thing from others. We came across some people, patients and healthy visitors, who asked to confirm the details about the nymph, requesting to see her. All the others who had come to check on the nymph were fathers and brothers of missing girls. They wanted to view the body in case she was their relative who was missing, had run away, or had been kidnapped. After entering and standing by the table where the nymph was laid out, each of them came away with nothing, not even their doubts. None of them ever again claimed to be the lover or relative of the headless girl. Different names and titles never stopped raining down on her from every side: the wife of the Shatt's servant, Satan's sacrifice, the lake bride, the otter's darling—the last one alluding to the nicks that otters had made on her body. But in the hospital's register, she was Fatima, with the American version of the name for an unidentified woman, Jane, placed in parentheses.

We opened the gate on our way, not disturbing the sleep of our inattentive guards. Rahlo pulled me close by the arm and whispered to me, "Father Emmo is a friend of mine—no, it's not what you think!" she said, cutting into the thought that ran through my mind. "He would enter our house from time to time, put a bundle in my hand, and move my fingers over it so I would know what it was. It was always a pile of books. He wanted to tell me that he didn't ask anything that the other men wanted. Then he would set about his task and pull my hand over to place it on the book covers. Not like others would do, who would pull my hand and place it on—"

Baghdadli interrupted by reaching over to grab at Rahlo's tongue, but Rahlo eluded her and burst out laughing. The blind prostitute described my father's labors: his examination of venereal diseases and the syphilis that was prevalent in those coastal brothels, the vials of mercury he would pour over the organs of increase (and other organs) of both men and women in order to heal them.

Baghdadli noticed that Rahlo was trying to get me to herself, and she wedged her body in between us, giving Rahlo's cheek a pinch that turned it red. Our visitor accompanied us as lightly as could be as we passed the small courtyard between the door of the hall and the hospital garden. From there she left us and walked on ahead, using the walls to guide herself, until she made herself comfortable in the examination chair in my father's office. Rahlo began by saying, "The first time I saw Father Emmo was at three o'clock in the morning one summer night. I sent a request to the hospital and came here barefoot, with some of my girls accompanying me. He told me my name was written in the friends registry." By *friends registry*, she meant the journal in which strangers recorded the names of their relatives or friends before lying down in the beds, listing the person the hospital should contact if something should happen to the patient, such as death or a coma. Since strangers did not know anyone in the city, they usually did not write a name, and the friends registry was empty except for fly dung. But it often happened that strangers would write the name *Rahlo*, the one name they remembered after a night of dissolution in her brothel. Therefore, I knew the name without knowing the identity of the person behind it. I read the name so often I initially thought it was the name of the village that the people came from, and I asked my father how far away Rahlo was.

Rahlo continued. "Your patients would write my name in the friends registry more than five times a month. How often your father delivered a corpse to me! I was never slow to come, not even when I didn't know them and scarcely remembered them. I had no connection to these people except that they wrote my name the previous night. I am the secret of the night." She suppressed her own laughter when she noticed we made no sound that suggested mirth. Then she added, her face gladdened by memories of Father Emmo, "I have a son named Janah, the fourth child to fill my belly and the only one who lived. All the others died on my bosom. One died after not getting enough to eat, while the other two got enough, but they drowned when the milk overflowed in their mouths and filled their nostrils. All except Janah. Father Emmo, that dervish in his colorful boat, gave me a copper mug, which I placed between my nipple and my baby Janah's nose. The mug was etched to look like a small golden palace. It had a notched handle so that I could tell by feeling it which way it was facing." I noticed Baghdadli smiling and nodding as Rahlo went on. "After Janah grew up, I gave this mug to my friends, and perhaps it has been passed around among them for a long time, passing through the hands of many a blind woman after me."

She began behaving as though she were in her favorite house. I was delighted when she pulled me over to the table. I might have resisted except for my passionate desire to see her entire face without any barriers. She had pulled away both her abayas and sat facing me, allowing me to examine the battleground of tattoos on her nose, her jaw, and her neck. I pondered them, imagining a tiger jumping out of her face and prowling for a while before finding its way into my bed, where it sniffed the walls, the sheets, and the damp spots scattered around the floor—all the blood, the sweat, and the spit. Then it stared at us with a nonchalant gaze and plopped down beside Rahlo like an obedient servant.

Shathra advanced and sat down cross-legged between me and Rahlo, behind whose eyes the tiger had peacefully retreated. The visitor repeated her question about the nymph. We told her that she had found her rest in the Evangelists Cemetery, which we gave Rahlo to understand was a row of graves beyond the Strangers Cemetery and was the site where we buried sisters and fathers from the team of evangelists. Baghdadli took an oath by Saint Ephrem so that Rahlo would believe her. Her tongue felt liberated to utter a saint she was not supposed to mention, neither him nor any others. During those women's evening conversations, she did not keep her tongue well bridled but returned for some minutes to her distant Assyrian Church and the initial curious enthusiasms of her youth. Then she caught herself, and she apologized in English—either to me or to the air—and once more, she was firmly ensconced in our church.

Then came a moment when none of us found anything to say. We were overcome by a bout of yawning that passed from one mouth to another. The brothel mistress lay back her head and stretched out her feet. I didn't want her to leave. Speaking for myself, I wanted neither her nor the present moment to move on. But Baghdadli began to fidget. She muttered some words without opening her lips. I liked their decorum when they were speaking about my father. I would have liked to speak to them, to be able to describe things without being limited to a pair of opposites, right and wrong: right for everything positive—the beautiful was *right*, the comfortable was *right*—and wrong for everything opposite them. My Arabic vocabulary was very weak at that time, and I did not possess many words to praise or criticize things. Everything was *right* or *wrong*. People never heard me using eloquent and exciting adjectives. Things of moderate goodness were *right*; odious matters were *wrong*. I didn't have sufficient words for my tongue to express precisely the thoughts circling through my mind. For example, when Rahlo asked us how Shathra was when in our company, I could only say, "Right." But Baghdadli said that Shathra was calm and obedient, and that while she had some shortcomings, she would soon learn and become quite clever. Before that session ended, when she gathered up her shawl and wrapped her abaya around her body again, Rahlo commented that I was sincere and that what was in my heart was on my tongue. "You English people speak straight as a ruler," she added. In reality, I was not using a ruler on my jawbone. All there was to it was that I only possessed some simple words, limited and impotent, too weak to describe everything. I felt the same thing with Baghdadli when she spoke to me in English. That ruler weighed down her tongue, and she lost the wealth of words she carried in her purse. In English, she moved her tongue within a narrow sphere, without making it say exactly what was in her head. She was unable to modulate her words and make them soft or rough. Even though I was envied to some degree by my peers and friends in Washington because I spoke more than one language, they did not realize that speaking a few words of some language may allow you to speak and be understood imprecisely, but it was like the difference between flying and limping. I was able to fly in English, while I limped in Arabic. I'm speaking now about the past, for today I can soar in both languages like a gull.

At the door, where we put her hand in Shathra's for them to go together to the sleeping quarters, Rahlo confided to us that my father used to stop in his colorful boat at the threshold of the brothel. He would greet everyone, and they would all raise a hand to him from afar. He would row more slowly to draw out the amount of time he spent passing them by, and more than once, he spent over an hour amid the smoke and vapors that spilled from the bellies of visitors, as well as the vile liquid that shot from them when they got drunk, became rowdy, and vomited. When they gathered in a circle around him, he would talk to them about the weather and the schedule of the tides. He did not drink or extend his hand to the tender flesh arrayed in front of him. Often, long, exhausting disputes would erupt among her visitors after he left. They would yell and curse at each other regarding the way others had interacted with him or greeted him. Rahlo's "daughters" might also take part in the dispute. That's the word Rahlo used for the prostitutes in her house. "There were these two young men," she said, "from among the group of men who were ranged along the walls, sitting with my daughters." She said those two men reached a dangerous degree of verbal squabbling regarding Father Emmo. The first worked as a porter for chests in a bottle factory; his name was not important. The important thing was that he kept criticizing the second one after he saw him shaking hands with my father, while the second one insisted that he was ready to drink water from the same cup Father Emmo had drunk from.

Rahlo continued. "The second swore on the heads of a thousand imams that he could kiss the English priest without a shudder. That is what made the first one shoot fire from his eyes. He shouted at the second that Father Emmo was a red gecko, another English unbeliever who corrupted the Gospels by erasing the name of Prophet Mohammed from them, who says that God sent his dick down through the clouds to penetrate the Virgin Maryam, the mother of His son. Every year, all their families gather in the church at the new year, extinguishing candles and closing the windows to spread utter darkness. Some of them lay with each other: brothers with sisters, mothers with sons-in-law. Then they dine on the flesh of swine—a filthy swine that lays with its sister. All that makes them unclean, and it's not permissible to touch them or shake hands with them." Rahlo stood up to act out the scene, showing how the first man had spat as he pictured his own state if it happened that he should touch Father Emmo. Then he said something that really angered the second, swearing by the heavens that touching the English caused the flesh to rot, afflicting it with blotching and warts, exactly the same after touching a frog. The second man, filled with rage, swore in front of everyone present that he would find Father Emmo to offer him a cup of water and that after Father Emmo had drunk his fill, he would drain the cup to the very last drop. Nay, he would even lick the rim! He asked the first man to accept a wager: "He would fulfill his promise in the eyes of all the people and under the disk of the sun. In exchange, he told the other man to pay him sixty qirsh if he did so. The wager was immediately accepted, and the two men made my girls their witnesses. But then the second man disappeared, and his promise became a subject of great and lasting mirth that kills people after their third glass."

Rahlo straightened up and gathered her leafy abaya from under her. I got down from my chair and sat leaning against Shathra, who stretched out her feet and vigorously scratched the broad cracks in her skin. She folded her legs and covered her feet back up as a gesture of respect when Rahlo dropped down beside her. Baghdadli was watching intently, as though writing everything on a chalkboard in her head. "The second disappeared, and we haven't seen him for a week and a half or so. My visitors and my girls relate that he has been seen in the market, where he tells people that he is still in the process of fulfilling his vow," Rahlo finished with a laugh.

One week had elapsed since my father's disappearance when Baghdadli and I decided to venture out, wearing the abayas of Mohammedan women as a disguise, something I repeated frequently afterward. It was not to search for my father, something that would have appeared to be the height of stupidity. We just walked for the sake of walking. We wanted to escape our existence there for a while and break free from the public image of the hospital team that was promulgated every month in the *Evangelical Journal*. By leaving behind our clothes, we broke out of that image, whose spiritual illnesses were always nearby, tucked underneath an armpit. Baghdadli proposed an excellent excuse that reduced the burden of guilt we felt for those dangerous nighttime excursions into a city where things did not seem quite right and where we had no idea what was coming. She suggested that we might come across the artificial leg as we wandered about, and we could ask about it. Asking people about Soldier Corbin's leg was safer than asking them about a missing priest.

As for how it reached the ears of Davenport that we were engaging in those nightly strolls, well, it could only be his spies, who "grew like mushrooms," for he did not only trade in wool, rolling it into a ball that spun far and wide, east and west, entangling nobles, imams in their mosques, date merchants, and even the loom weavers who were scattered along the roads. One night, as we opened the door to slip into our beds, we found him sprawled across the floor, reading the newspaper and drawing lines and circles as he twisted his mustache. He did not raise his face from the page, nor did his pen stop circling, as he said, "Tomorrow, at first light, I'll drive out Shathra." That was not the full punishment. We were surprised at the morning communion service when six guards stood in an impregnable line at the gate of the hospital. Baghdadli noticed that I crawled as quickly as I could in their direction. She was afraid of my anger, being well aware of its consequences. I was not one of those people who could control the volcano inside them when it exploded. She ran toward me and stopped me, wrapping me in her arms. She knew without a doubt that I would go out to the guards and strike them, latching on to their legs like tongs. I might even have gone over to Davenport and spat on him. She herself had previously observed what came of my fits of rage. I would pour them out against the hospital curtains, with their revolting slime color, by pulling them down off all the windows. Then the bald, melancholy sun would slip through the openings with all its light to startle the eyelids of the patients and disturb their slumber.

It happened once that they tied me up as I writhed as though possessed, cursing everyone, even my father—who, at that time, had prevented me from writing to the magazine on account of a response he had received from the editorial staff. They had advised him to supervise my writings and my drafts until he had more time to develop my character and guide me on the sound path of controlling my pen—for not everything we saw and knew was appropriate to be written—and so on and so forth, together with other advice from the magazines that I had memorized by heart.

I submitted to Baghdadli's fingers as she gripped my rib cage as though I were a chicken. Davenport's fingers seized the back of my neck. Then he began to stroke it, and I grew calm. I felt as though I were an otter that yawns as it relaxes under the hand of a deceptive hunter. I do not deny that they curbed my nervous rebellion that day, nor do I deny that it made me feel relieved, since regret often overpowered me when I remembered what I lost to those furies of mine.

"I know that you published a report in the magazine about my father and I returning," I said with excessive amiability, either feigned on my part or engendered by my fear—I don't know which. It was as though I were certain that this man would get rid of me: he would make the news come true. I expected him to change his tone, which was empty of all emotion, and to receive me with an affectionate response. What actually happened was that he pulled back a little from me. He brushed the hem of his pants to knock off some dirt. Then he put his staff under his arm as he replied, "When someone invents a treatment for the disease of composing stories, I will be the first to buy it. We'll put it in a dropper to rinse your eyes and wash your tongue. In my entire life, which has taken me both east and west, I've never found anyone who uses writing the way you do. You write like a man. And not just any man! But the kind who's good at nothing but words and stroking his oiled mustache. Words, words like dead fish diffusing all the rottenness of the world. You carry them out to throw at people, and they run from you. Shouldn't writing be a sweet act that reflects respect for ourselves and for others? Why do you write putrid words? Why must we allow you to put them in our pockets? Why did your instruction in writing and the permission you received to fabricate stories become such a dangerous act that would turn into shame for everyone who knows you? Christ alone knows how much Father Emmo will suffer from this escape of yours. That is, if he hasn't already died or lost his mind on account of a daughter . . . three-quarters of a daughter, that is, like some kind of nightmare." He exhaled loudly through his nose before suddenly cutting off the air and going on. "Why don't you comb your hair like other girls? I also wish to see you in a dress rather than these bulbous trousers of yours."

"By the way," he told me, during another of his outbursts, which did not cease even after that day, "it wasn't me who sent that report to the newspaper."

THE OVERLEAF SOCIETY

The faces of the six guards were not strange since they were all patients at Strangers Hospital.

Davenport offered them that opportunity to work, and they left their beds for shifts at the door. They guarded it, for who was more appropriate to protect Strangers Hospital than the strangers of that hospital?

As a result, it was very easy to embroil them in our affairs. These patients were saints of pious dissembling. They were rough and severe guards at the hospital gate in the presence of Davenport and all his spies and sources. But they were our patients, so they colluded with our absence, never refusing to open the door for us when we went out in our Mohammedan abayas at night. Each time, Baghdadli charged Madelena to bring them vegetable soup and carrot bread, followed by cups of glorious Yemeni coffee, the beans of which she ground and roasted in their shells over the firepit. Baghdadli made the sign of the cross in front of them so many times that they abandoned their smiles at seeing us in those abayas and banished from their imagination the idea that we had renounced our own religion because we were wearing the clothes of another.

After going out, we would slowly make our way to the bowers of Rahlo's brothel. We threw stones or date pits until she came out to us, most often drunk and leaning on one of her girls. After getting into the boat with her, she would rouse herself from the intoxication. She only pretended to be drunk among her visitors in order to kill the boredom in their souls. Shathra, who was prevented from seeing us at the hospital, joined her after hearing Baghdadli's voice and the knocking sound our feet made as we got into the boat. Earlier, Rahlo had promised us she would report everything that passed the lips of her clients and slipped accidentally from their tongues, especially the man who'd made the wager and any developments in his emphatic vow to drink from a cup polluted by my father's saliva. We would talk as we traced lines through the water in her boat, lit up by a red lantern, its fire dancing and gleaming in the steam of the end of the night. We whispered to her, and she whispered to us.

"That young man who made the wager is called Bansar, Ring Finger, and he is part of the Overleaf Society," said Rahlo. It was not the first time I had heard the name of the Overleaf. I had the idea that they were a group of scribes, whose number did not exceed the fingers on one hand. They were afflicted by what my father called a frenzy of writing. He refused to call it an illness. Rather, it was an addiction that resembled an illness, an addiction to practice calligraphy day and night. Some of them even did so while complaining about pain in their neck vertebrae, the blood being cut off in their fingers, or their wrist joint not working properly. As for why the people called them the Overleaf Society, it was because they only wrote on the back of government papers, receipts for grains and dates, custom papers, letters, and annals. There was no other way to describe them. Perhaps it was because they were cheap or poor that they used the backs of other pages to practice that filthy habit of theirs.

I asked Baghdadli if she could describe their faces. "No one has seen their faces," she replied. "Wherever they go, they wrap their faces or disguise themselves in various clothes."

Rahlo was quick to say that wasn't the case at all. They disguised themselves, but everyone knew what they looked like. "Perhaps they take extra care with the disguises in front of you so they appear to be important people. They might also take the disguises seriously if they are afraid of their families, their mothers in particular. Most of these scribes have been driven from their home and their tribe." As for their tribe, the Overleaf Society was drawn from the sons of pashas and the chiefs of the tribes, or they were sons of wealthy families whose palaces and strongholds were scattered along the Shatt. They studied in Istanbul at Ashirat Maktabi School, which the sultan had designated for sons of nobility and the wealthy in order to educate them to become directors of offices in their own country. Some of them traveled to Paris and brought back a Frenchman's clothes, hat, and large umbrella to the land of plentiful palm trees and sunshine. They mixed with those visiting from Europe or English cities—from "beyond the seven seas," as the blind prostitute put it. They wandered through the markets and the reception halls of hotels, sheikhs, consulates, and libraries of the big ships, where some of them worked as secretaries and guardians of the books and newspapers. That was the case in the best of circumstances, for they quickly lost those positions after proprietors, directors, and ship captains discovered their propensities and question-raising habits, replete with errors and dissolute morals. They classified themselves as a secret society that inherited the disease of writing and passed down the banner from generation to generation. It was said that the first five of them emerged when Alexander the Great visited Basra in the mists of time. They recorded that famous visit in great detail and precision, like an artist's portrait. But for them, the history of events was a byproduct. They were not interested in history: it just dripped off their fingers automatically. The need to practice calligraphy meant a need for words, and whoever did not have words drew from the speech of the people. The secret was that they did not stop writing. Therefore, they recorded everything that passed through their ears. In that way, they preserved the rush of their exhausting exercises for writing and conveying their exceeding pleasure for recording, which was followed by intoxication. Across the centuries and the ages, they were not satisfied with the talk of the people, so they added events. The most famous things that happened among them became fruit for their fingers, which never tired and never grew bored.

Rahlo said, “One day, the faithful sent them out of the mosque with a foot on the backside after the Overleaf Society objected to a religious story that dated back to ancient times. They denounced it as a lie and backed up their words with evidence from the backs of documents. Denunciations and cries went up before their ribs were cracked under the feet of youths, and angry women defended the religion with their teeth. When the people trapped them in an alley and laid into them, this society turned and defended themselves with extreme savagery, which led people to start calling them a gang. As usual, all these convulsions and convocations dispersed when the Qawnaq police arrived. The people pretended that nothing was happening. The beater and the beaten, the oppressor and the wounded: all disappeared, blending into the crowd. The people worked together—the aggressor and the aggressed upon, the onlookers and the neutral parties—in concocting a story for the police, with everyone protecting each other.”

Shathra interrupted by striking her thigh to let us know she wanted to speak, not having found any space to insert her voice into that discussion, which needed quick tongues supplied with the spirit of exaggeration. She spoke and finished what she had to say. Then she tried to repeat what she had said, starting over from the beginning with lighter words. She noticed that her heavy voice and swollen tongue could not push out the words as they ought, but we put our hands over her mouth, and she fell silent. She pushed away our hands, twisting them behind our shoulders, and we cried out in pain. She opened our lantern and spit upon it until it went out. Darkness filled the boat. Then dawn burst from Rahlo’s breast. I caught myself smiling unconsciously when the locks on the nape of her neck shimmered as they fell in waves over her eyes. A stillness fell that allowed Shathra to clear her throat and resume telling her story about the Overleaf Society: “I watched some of them at sunset, squatting on the walls of the Qawnaq palace, gathering the scraps of paper that fly out the windows, from the barges pulled by donkeys, and garbage that the guards bury. They gathered them up, turned them over, and began writing on them."

Rahlo told of an incident that happened when she was four years old. The shore echoed with screams and cries to God. Crowds of vendors and shopkeepers in the market advanced, going down to the water. The voices of the faithful in the neighboring Porters Mosque died away. A mail packet ship crossing the Gulf and bound for the Mediterranean had gone up in a great blaze. The fire seized bundles of letters and papers belonging to the people—to travelers, to emperors, and to kings. Rahlo interlaced her fingers over her head and said, "Most of the people could be seen interlacing their fingers atop their heads in anguish, like this." Travelers and residents observed the people's words, their news, and their greetings to family rising in a column of white smoke. The wind blew half of it away as ash, and the water swallowed the other half, carrying it off to the city on the current. That was the most blessed of days for those who gathered papers and scraps. It was the first festival of the Overleaf Society, when the Shatt supplied them with a never-ending supply of empty spaces to store up their words and their days, which no one has ever read.

The agreement with Baghdadli was that we would keep our lips sealed on anything related to the nobleman who made the wage and the five-fold guild known as the Overleaf Society. If God should grant that we acquire a list of their names and addresses, that would remain a closely guarded secret, kept away from the men of the Qawnaq and those around them, and especially from Davenport. I promised her I would behave more intelligently this time and keep a rein on my anger. The light of dawn brightened the sky. Porters pushed their tired three-wheeled carts, singing songs about going home, and we felt no fear for them. But I was literally trembling on account of the pedestrians among them, who walked slowly and took advantage of the convenient opportunities to address us. As for the cart drivers, they caught our eyes quickly, but any danger from them passed in seconds. They did not stop, nor did they pull Baghdadli's abaya or my golden braids. I remember that one of the workers kept close to us, walking at the same pace and rhythm and keeping a consistent distance between him and us. We turned and saw him scowling in a rubbery smile, even when Baghdadli addressed me in a way that he would hear and said, "We will grill a ewe's head on your ears and make you a spectacle for the people." That did not turn the man away, and he kept swaggering with arms crossed, in his thick wooden clogs and a silk sash that floated from his shoulder. He carried a bundle in his hand; no doubt it was his work clothes, which he had taken off after finishing his shift when he decided to go down to the Shatt to look for women.

At that moment, when that man was nearly on top of us, Davenport appeared, shocking and dismaying me. Baghdadli adopted the dignified air she put on only in Davenport's presence. He held his ground, blocking the way between us and the man. We pushed forward gently to get home quicker while the man began explaining and showering Davenport with greetings and friendly questions about his health. Then he reached out his hand to shake, even though greetings in that city were not a matter of putting hands or noses together, but consisted of laying heads on each other's shoulders for a few minutes until two rivers join in concord between you—two rivers of sweat, that is.

We moved back a little, watching the two men. Davenport took out his wallet, which hung below his chest under his shirt as though it were a bitch's teat. He drew from it an Ottoman lira, and its colors shone in the eye of the clog seller. Davenport handed it over, pressing it into the man's hand, which he folded over the note. The man was astonished and bobbed his knees several times. He struck his chest twice, and from a distance, it appeared that he launched into a string of expressions of embarrassment and deep obligation. Despite the man's protests, Davenport insisted that he take the lira, threatening to add a second if he wouldn't take just one. Davenport kept increasing the number of liras the more the man insisted bashfully that he could not take them and denied his shameful deed. In the end the amount reached five liras, which might equal six months of his salary for working at sea. Davenport stuffed them into a belt running around the man's waist. Then he withdrew and took up a position at the wooden bridge suspended from palm trunks. I was surprised that Davenport would pay a man who had made us feel so frightened. I cursed him in a whisper, and Baghdadli joined me in repeating the same curse. We wrapped ourselves again in our abayas. Davenport joined us, letting us know that he would protect us and, indeed, that he did not care about the way we violated the new rules laid down by the assistant deputy vice consul after the disappearance of my father. He would just appear out of nowhere each time and give a handful of liras to anyone who harassed us.

He asked us to stop alongside, and we picked a corner under the Nestorian church, which looked like one of the churches of the north that Baghdadli had come from. It would have been an unhappy moment had the acolytes there recognized her entering the church in the garb of Mohammedan women. They would have thought that the former prioress had converted from Orthodox Assyrian Church to American Protestantism and then to Mohammedanism, and that the Lord alone knew the form of the next god on the list of her aspirations. She laughed. Then she burped as she told me how she imagined her relatives saying that. And it's a good thing that she covered her face entirely and used me as her eyes. We turned around and did not find Shathra. She was afraid of Davenport, who would drive her away whenever the opportunity presented itself. After we had been standing there a long time, we asked him the reason we were waiting there. He just asked us to wait and to watch closely, pointing with his chin at the young man in the clogs and the silk sash. We did not have to wait much longer. A group of women passed in front of the bridge, and the young man leaped out at them. He addressed them with some particularly offensive propositions and reached out toward them. The women fled, and in the same moment, three men swooped down upon the man with the sash. It appeared that the women were accompanied by family guardians, who quickly turned the young man into a lake of blood and guts that spilled from a large gash in his belly. They spread him over the ground as though spreading fish under the sun to be dried and salted, without needing to smoke them first.

We could only admire Davenport for his shrewdness and curse him for his bloodthirstiness. Knowing the fatal risk it entailed, Davenport had encouraged the young man to touch the women, insinuating that doing so would bring him a shower of money, both qirsh and lira. Without offering Davenport the gratitude he was expecting from us, we turned silently in the direction of the hospital.

The next day, we hurriedly gathered the people we would charge to search for my leg with Shathra. I entrusted to her the major task of overseeing their routes and paths through the city. I undertook making a sketch of my leg on paper. I repeated the drawing seven times, handing it out to them with exhaustive commentaries in dialects they understood. They departed, and we made the sign of the cross over their footsteps. Baghdadli did not lose this golden opportunity to call upon her saints, who were forbidden in Strangers Hospital. She prayed at the gate as she watched the phantoms of the workers searching for my father disappear among the almond trees. She opened her hand and stood regarding her palm, murmuring, "O Father Khando! O saint of innocence! O intercessor for desperate needs! Just as you have never failed someone who pleads with you to attain his desperate need, I now ask you to restore the leg of this young lady, spotted with freckles. I know you are lazy, and you spend your day skipping through the valleys in search of children's stuffed dolls. You move your ass among the churches, riling up the solitary monk in the deserts, the wastelands, and the mountains. You pluck off their hats and knock their crosses to the floor. You pound on the doors of their cells and caves and then run away. What an irksome, disgusting child you are, with a miserly disposition. Your naughtiness exceeds all bounds, and the people call upon your father Jesus to punish you. All you do is fall to the ground laughing because you know that in your innocence, you are God's beloved. He pampers you, and He does not grant the people's imputations against you. Blessed be your glory when your fickle, bubbling laughter rises high. I adjure you by your mother and your father! Come! Restore the leg of this stranger! If you deny you stole her leg, I won't be upset with you. Given how long you've made off with my precious things and my small family reserves, just restore the leg for the good of it. We won't curse you. We won't neglect our vows to you. I will buy you mutton for a glorious banquet and invite the poor to join you. If only you show your beneficence and restore our leg!"

"Who is Khando?" I asked Baghdadli. The question fell like ice upon her flaming genius.

In the ancient city of Assur, Khando was a child of three years when his parents announced that they would follow Jesus. They were thrown in prison along with many others and subjected to innumerable bouts of burning and whipping, with wrenching of their fingers and limbs. After the king's daughter and her brother announced they would join Jesus, too, like some of the common people, Khando was torn away from his parents in prison and made to drink boiling water. But not even that made him abandon the Holy King. Then a miracle took place. Khando spoke and prayed like a full-grown adult, prepared for the glory of meeting the Lord. The king's myrmidons mounted the palace stairs with him and threw him down from halfway up. He landed headfirst on the paving stones and went straight to heaven. Afterward, however, he began appearing in people's dreams and in their thoughts, among the trees, and through the windows. He helped them meet needs they had forgotten or despaired of. He was famous in the books of monks as the saint of troublemakers, as having a child's heart and a simple faith.

On the same day Baghdadli told me this story, I saw a man with baggy trousers and a white jacket that revealed the hair on his belly. He was chanting inside the hospital pharmacy, where Baghdadli was accustomed to spending two hours every day. He was carrying a round case that was puffed up at its top and came to a point at its bottom, as though it were the trunk of a pregnant tree. The man had placed a towel over his bald head, which gleamed with oil and sweat, in order to ward off a swarm of gnats. Baghdadli had never before received a man and closed the door on the two of them so that they were out of sight. Therefore, their sitting alone together aroused my curiosity. Using the wheelchair my father had made for me out of wood, tin, and rubber wheels, I moved toward them and kicked the door. The man stood up and bowed to greet me. He seemed gracious and had a warm smile. Baghdadli introduced him to me: "This is my brother, Khando." When she saw the wonder lighting up my face, she smiled and clicked her tongue.

"Yes, we named him after the saint of lost earrings."

"Just earrings?" I said, expressing my dissatisfaction at the name since it suggested that the leg of the Soldier Corbin was not among his specialties.

So Khando was her younger brother. He was the man in the picture pressed inside the book of hymns and prayers that she carried in a leather bag she never parted with. He was her one remaining intimate link to the family home, where the cold pillows had not thawed ever since Father Emmo had entangled her in a different church.

Khando had been a hymn chanter in the Assyrian Church. Then he was caught up by the military draft and worked as a military chorister, singing battalion anthems in the Ottoman army to the north of the city. On his last long leave, he had acquired a musical instrument, a kind of pregnant guitar called an oud. He found one, thrown face down among the goods for sale from a ship that had sunk or needed to reduce its cargo. When the oud had not found a buyer, Khando walked barefoot that day, cradling his wooden child, dirty with sea grass, to his chest. He disappeared from everyone's eyes, including the church choir composed of his female cousins and the wives of his siblings and their children. He occupied himself with composing other songs, similarly melancholic.

But he failed to sell them to the tavern singers and decided to continue practicing in the hopes of living one day from the fruits of his oud.

His sister presented me. "This is Charlotte, a clever girl who sends letters to the magazines that are important enough for the editors to publish, along with their responses. She's the daughter of Father Emmo."

He appeared anxious with longing as he recalled my father. He reminded his sister that no one could forget the priest's boat, as he cleaved the Shatt faster than a man running, as though he were an experienced oarsman.

"Nice to meet you!" he said, running his eyes down to my feet and back up to my neck, where the bullet necklace gleamed. I was watching the blue stones on the rings on his fingers as he spread them over his thighs, sitting with his sister on a thick rug that rose a few inches off the ground, seemingly untroubled by the smell of medicine all around him. Khando commented on my necklace, the necklace of the water nymph. He praised its design and its shine. His sister confirmed for him that she'd rubbed the shell of the bullet until the brass gleamed. After that, I began chattering without stop. I let the entire story pour from my lips—everything I knew about the water nymph, along with everything I didn't.

THE ZURKHANEH LION

After the telegram arrived from the magazine *Evangelism* in New York, Davenport sent it to me with the delivery man. The telegram was a reply to an inquiry sent by Davenport, requesting information about the identity of the person who had sent the false news of the journey, and the reply came back as follows: "On November 13, a short letter reached the Smith House Post Office in Seattle from Mr. Emmanuel B. R., director of the evangelical mission of Arabia in Basra, requesting that we publish the news of his return, together with his daughter, Charlotte, aboard the steamship *Sakandwand.* He would be prepared to attend church meetings, write sermons, and receive visits starting one month after the date of his arrival. Also mentioned was the date of the trip, down to the very minute of arrival; the address of the harbor; and the name of the dock, which would bring him to us overland from the Gulf of Mexico this time and not the Hudson Bay, as with his past voyages." After the reply came the magazine's notice that it would cease publication until further notice. It did not provide any reason, but there was no need, since all the evangelicals in Arabia had been following the news of events in Washington and how conditions were throughout the rest of the country. Demonstrations made up of the unemployed had turned into an army without guns that might march upon the capitol. Farmers back home had realized that burning their corn was cheaper than selling it; banks had started raising the interest rates on the loans taken out by churches; silver mines had closed their galleries; hunger decimated the wealthy even before the indigent; and the cry on the tongues of the demonstrators repeated the words of the poor, which were used in speeches in congress. My return journey with my father, the journey that was never taken: by the time the telegram arrived, two weeks had passed since that trip was said to have taken place. Yet Father Emmo was only in the magazine, neither in America nor in Basra. He had disappeared, only to reappear between the lines and under the torn edges of its pages. I felt a heightened sense of compassion for the father who existed in the magazine, the written father, who had apparently fabricated the news of our return. Then he split into two fathers, one written and one lost: the written one embalmed in the magazine as he sailed aboard the steamship; and the other, who was gone. In doing so, he had divided me along with him. Apparently, daughters can be bifurcated along with their fathers.

During one of our days together in Basra, I was working to get a hair out of my mouth while my father was talking with me. I wasn't paying attention to him, busy scratching at my face and trying to pop some pimples, when he suddenly knelt before me. "I want to make an alliance with you, Charlotte." The word *alliance* woke me up when he uttered it. Who was this priest down on his knees? Right, it was my father, Emmanuel, known to everyone here as Father Emmo. His sentence seized my attention entirely, and I was gripped with curiosity about why my father had to make an alliance with his seated daughter, especially since that term always had a bad connotation for me, something he himself had taught me, exactly six years before, when the ships of the Indian Ocean set out with us from Zanzibar to Basra. I heard him deep in a tense conversation with a random passenger. The sixteen yellow buttons distributed across the other man's shirt suggested that he was French, while the damp flush of his cheeks declared that he was drunk. To make a long story short, that sharp dispute ended with a swelling that looked like a nipple on my father's cheek after the Frenchman dealt him a sudden blow that knocked him to the deck of the ship, crumpled like a winter coat that had fallen off its hook.

The French nuns who were with us on the same ship appeared without any preliminaries and set about tending to my father. Meanwhile, people gathered round me, patting my shoulder and gazing at me sorrowfully. I hovered over my father, unable to lift him up and support his weight. In that conversation, both the inebriated Frenchman and my father mentioned the word *alliance* from one sentence to the next. As far as I could make out, the Frenchman was furious about what was known as the Alliance of the Lily and the Crescent Moon, which was the agreement, ratified centuries earlier and subsequently renewed, between the rulers of his country and the Ottoman sultans, who ruled the Mohammedan world, for the sake of protecting the French missionaries and priests in the lands of Arabia and allowing Christians to pass safely through Mohammedan lands and vice versa. The angry Frenchman had indignantly called it "an alliance that sullied the admirable lily with the crescent." The chattering nuns said that this man with the fist that didn't miss was a doll merchant, the kind used by Parisian fashion designers to showcase dresses, bras, bows, nylons, and men's jackets. In addition, his family was famous for their expansive mercantile activities. They supplied theaters with various costumes, such as Turkish sultans and generals, so that the actors could make fun of them onstage in their comedy performances. After the alliance, they were forced to show respect to the sultans and were prevented from making them the butt of their jokes and humorous sketches because that would mean the French would be exposed to things that would not end well in the sultan's lands. The Frenchman, who managed the business accounts for his family, had been forced to stop producing dolls of the sultans and their clothing in his family's workshop. A bout of drunken tippling led him into conversation with my father, which he began by saying, "Do you know the best way to drink until the break of day without vomiting?" My father didn't reply. "You don't know, do you? It's by staying up to converse with an American priest!" My father was the only American priest on that steamship, and they got to speaking. One idea led to another until they came in the end to that alliance, which my father praised. It cost him a bloody nose and a nipple on his cheek that lived before my eyes for days.

Besides that alliance, my father and I had another one that we called "the Fart Treaty," which allowed each of us to pass gas in the presence of the other at any time, so long as it was only the two of us, with no one else present, without either of us needing to notify the other before doing so.

He later came to me about another alliance that was not yet sullied and would not ruin any mode of commerce. He knelt before me and explained to me its terms: "I will not close my eyes until I see you happy. I will be the shade that protects your shade. Indeed, I will stroke it, rub it, and sterilize it every day." He looked embarrassed when mentioning the topic of sterilization. Perhaps his tongue betrayed him and slipped toward embarrassing allusions that he certainly had not meant. For I do not think he was referring to the thick odor that assaulted him whenever he opened my drawers for some reason. I myself choked on the stench of blood, pus, and ammonia that emanated from there. It didn't even help that I had gotten used to it. Now his alliances represented a somewhat painful idea. He and his alliances had vanished, along with his smiles, the sound of his snoring, and his cracking knuckles. With my father gone, I was left behind to clean the windows of the vomit and spit that patients deposited there, which they launched when they saw their noses swelling up on account of the mosquitoes and the wicked sweat of the coast. And perhaps he left me with the worst poison of all, which is when you have to pretend to miss someone, or at least to be simpleminded. That seemed to be the lesson he had wanted to teach when he talked to me after I finished reading the play *Hamlet*. At that time, he emphasized the character of Hamlet's beloved, Ophelia, whose father disappeared. All she could do was transform into a crazy person, scattering garlands of laurel wherever she went and wandering, lost in her fantasies, until she died by drowning, heartsick for her father.

From an early age, my father planted inside me the character of young Ophelia, crying for her vanished father.

On the afternoon when the magazine's telegram arrived, I crawled over to the wheelchair that my father had built for me. Without pausing to put a shawl over my head, I wheeled myself outside, struggling with the bumps in the dirt road leading to the Shatt. Before I even saw her coming, Baghdadli approached and picked me up to carry me where I wanted to go. I liked to go and sit on a large boulder, which was actually the remains of a failed rocket that had been fired by the Turkish garrison during their successive wars with the Ajak, who descended upon the Arabian Gulf and the holy graves in that region, which was shaped like a funnel on the sultan's map. The rocket sprouted here, petrified, and was now older than the palm trees. The people called it Abu Kishra, meaning *the Grimacer*. Abu Kishra was a little taller than three times my height; there was no exact estimate for the part buried under the soil. The important thing was that it stood erect, like a pale lighthouse at night and like a sundial driving away the sun during the day. It had acquired a bad reputation, especially after lovers were observed sitting atop it with limbs intertwined. From a great distance, the viewer saw their bodies interlocked, pressing together and trembling. Before long, however, the rocket had reclaimed its dignity, and that was when Shathra urinated around it, like a lioness fencing in her bower and claiming possession of a certain spot. I used to go there to laugh and trade dirty jokes with Shathra and Baghdadli, but that day, I went there to laugh and cry in Baghdadli's company, who took the water nymph's necklace in order to scratch a verse on it, using a pin she had scoured in sand and sharpened on the brass of a bullet: *Jesus watches over us, like a father over his children.* I leaned my thigh against Baghdadli's knee. Embracing her slowly, I whispered, "But I'm fifteen years old today." I wanted a verse that matched my size, or else for us to write a longer verse on a slip of paper and stuff it inside the hollow of that necklace.

"'Unless you become like little children once again, you shall not enter the kingdom of heaven.'" Baghdadli recited the verse and leaned her head against Abu Kishra. She dozed off before beginning to write on the bullet.

I took out the telegram and shoved it inside Baghdadli's pocket. She startled awake when my hand was pressed deep inside her clothing, as though the message from the New York magazine, which had come out hot from the mailbag, were burning her. She picked me up and carried me away from the stone rocket. Lowering me down onto the bank of the river, she threw her abaya over me. I knew she wanted me to urinate. She was unable to carry me to the bathroom in the hospital, and the fresh air and its smell would have been pleasant for her were I not polluting it with the fumes of my bladder.

Then we went back to the hospital gate, slowed by a long line of pregnant women. It was a common sight in those days: the pregnant bellies lining up after a journey of six or seven months and filled with the fetuses planted there by fishermen, fathers who stored up and aged their juices a long time before going back to their women after exhausting searches for migrating fish that they'd hurried to catch before they fell into the nets of others. These fishermen caught them young and in great numbers before they separated into the various branches of the Shatt, where they grew larger but diminished in number. According to my father, the ilish fish was a sort of measurement that allowed those sailing into the Arabian Gulf to know the conditions of life in the city even before they dropped anchor. More precisely, they could tell by the females, who returned from the sea into the freshwater rivers to lay their eggs. If the fish were small, that meant the city was thriving and had not suffered any catastrophes. But if they were large, that meant the city had suffered a plague and most of its residents had died, granting the females a respite from the fishermen. They ate their fill and grew fat while their bellies filled with eggs.

Baghdadli scratched her cheek. This crowd in front of the hospital was not safe. It had not previously happened that such a large number of pregnant women had gathered around us. I announced my anger by pulling down on Baghdadli's shawl. I watched as her cheeks sucked in, her eyes rolled back, and her silver locks tumbled down over her cheeks until they appeared to get caught in the hairs extending from her flared nostrils. Nevertheless, she just kept smiling and reassuring the crowd as though they were her patients, even though they weren't sick. It was not natural for a pregnant girl to turn up at Strangers Hospital. She would be exposed to problems since her presence here might suggest to women that she'd become pregnant through fornication or that it was a foreign baby from a foreign father. As a result, these lines were usually small and subdued. Yet they had grown enormous that day, as these women gathered to seek our help. The pleading turned into unintelligible words, boastful and repugnant. They were asking us for any relics of the water nymph. We did not know what magic spell had exhorted them to do that. It had never before happened that someone demanded a piece from the bodies of those who had died in the hospital.

One of them nearly tore the gate off its hinges. The nose of another was being squeezed so hard between bars of the gate and the crowd of bodies that I expected her fetus to shoot out, swimming in its liquids among their feet, like a shooting pit when you squeeze a date between your fingers. Perhaps she kept it in by clenching her body's openings and holding her breath, for none of them wanted to bear her child among us. It would not help any of them for it to be said that her child was a bastard born at Strangers Hospital. All their hopes were joined, and all throats were calling out. They cried out for Madelena and Baghdadli. My father's name was also mentioned, for the news of his disappearance had not fully made the rounds. They screamed at us, calling the names of all the evangelical men and daughters who had passed through that place, even those who had died. We informed them that the nymph had been raised out of the water naked, so there were no traces of clothes or the like. They asked for anything that had touched her and everything that had been cut off her. Hadn't that translucent body left behind a tuft of hair or a fleck of skin?

Baghdadli committed one of her more thoughtless actions, which very rarely happened for her, when she agreed to my suggestion. I told her we should bring out the sheet that had covered the water nymph on the day she was laid out on the table. Baghdadli applied herself to my idea and brought the sheet out to them. The women rushed upon it like starving vultures, and in a matter of seconds, the sheet, which was embroidered with the head of a horse wearing a crown, was turned into the tiniest of scraps. The sheet was no longer able to give them anything, nor could we give away our scalpels, calipers, flasks, and brushes, all those instruments that were impossible to replace in a situation like ours. Baghdadli shared what she came to learn from the less fanatical women in the line, which is that they desired the help of the water nymph's relics in order to bear male children. There was a rumor circulating that walking on the relics of a harlot who was killed by her tribe to defend their honor would bring a male child. They waited patiently for instances of the curse to revert to the murdered girl, allowing their fetuses to be changed into boys. A male child did not inspire anyone's aversion, and it protected a woman from the burden of insults and the prattle of bachelors ranged along the bridges.

The women thronged around us. The sheet did not disperse them, nor did our pleas that they withdraw. It was at this point, as always happened, that Shathra's head hatched a trick to bring an end to that tedious day. Shouldering the weight of her body toward the gate, she made the bellies around her start shaking, together with their contents. Forming a barrier that prevented them from entering, she thrust them away from the fence. Then she opened the bag made from the folds in her dress and began scattering its contents upon the bank. The white cubes she was throwing looked like bits of fat fed to stray cats. I later realized she was throwing molars, large teeth that were bloody and decayed. It was a handful of the ones my father had extracted from people's mouths. The teeth flew from her pocket, and women plunged, headlong and fully clothed, into the Shatt to snatch the teeth from the air before they touched the water. Their pitch-black hair floated on the surface. Their heads dipped in the water had the effect of pouring out a glass of oil, forming a patch of whale secretions—which was widely used in women's hair—that diffracted into a bundle of colors. When the dust had settled at the end of the battle, each of the faces of those who won the nymph's teeth were adorned by a fierce smile, the smile of someone who had just been delivered of a male child who dropped to the ground between her legs. Those teeth weren't the actual teeth of the water nymph; Shathra had just collected them from the trash. Yet the women had no reason to doubt that they weren't something left behind by the water nymph. A passing male ibis swept down to the ground, hunting out a molar that had slipped through someone's fingers. It stole the tooth and rose into the naked sky. The women took that as a dazzling sign of the spiritual power of the water nymph's body.

During all that commotion, Davenport was waiting at the door of the mosque for Kadhim Pasha to emerge, carried on his litter in front of his retinue, which followed him like a line of penguins, each of whom bore a gold-and-turquoise dagger that bounced on his belly. The assistant deputy vice consul watched for the wali's approach and prevented his feet from progressing even an inch inside the mosque. He did not want to repeat his previous disaster when entering a mosque. The first time he'd set foot in this city of Basra, he followed a line of praying men and went into the mosque with them, only to have everyone flee his presence before the guards drove him out with their shoes. He deserved the curses, the kicks, and the suspicious looks, which prompted the person who delivered the Friday sermon, Sheikh Qasim, who was known as the Rooster, to cram Davenport into his list of vituperations and daily curses, which included all religious adversaries and the enemies of God, including his brother-in-law, his mother-in-law, and his sister-in-law. Davenport was described in the Rooster's sermon as being a pilfering Englishman with a mustache that was red from dipping so often in wine. He was meddlesome and stupid, and he crawled rather than walked. The latter was a reference to Davenport's manner of walking, for this ponderous merchant was afraid that his blue shoes would be damaged by the stones, and he moved his feet with excessive, unnecessary care. With his entry into the Friday sermon, Davenport became part of the general description of the city and, specifically, the ranks of the wicked.

But the Rooster's sermon was made of sand, not words.

The situation changed, and the Rooster began mentioning Davenport by his full natural name, followed by the color of his beard and his shoes, together with terms of praise, a prayer for his success and payments of his trade accounts and his generosity to his brothers. For, as he said, all of us were branches from the tree of Adam, who drove us from paradise while we were still in his loins so that we might get to know each other, become acquainted, and come to love each other.

As he listened to the Rooster's words, Davenport hugged a long ledger under his arm, only a little shorter than the man himself. He always strutted along with that notebook. It was a sail he used to catch the wind, and it carried him like the staff he sometimes leaned upon. In its yellowed pages were crammed columns of accounts, dates, signatures, seals, and notations; stamps made from sesame halva and flavored with nutmeg, which he liked, purchased from itinerant women. A crowded logbook with no space inside for a new line, and no hope for using it to record any transaction. Nevertheless, he carried it to keep his body in equilibrium as he walked through the markets, for without it, he was powerless to act natural and avoid drawing unwanted attention.

He took up a position in a shady corner and bowed his head as he listened to the Rooster's admonitions. What he had not expected was that the Rooster would not mention him in the least this time, neither to rebuke him nor to praise him. The man's gullet, much like the crop of his namesake, was as capacious as the ebb and flow of the tides. It was a measure of the feelings of warmth, displeasure, or acceptance that the wali harbored for him. Most people listened to his sermon in order to gauge that degree of warmth, as well as anything it suggested regarding other notables. They would ignore his way of speaking and its illogical connection to his subjects. They would ignore his voice—a voice that did not suit his noble and dignified face, soft and coquettish, which for so long had enticed fishermen, travelers, and sailors visiting the city for the first time. His sermon found its way to their ears, and because they did not understand the Arabic, they thought it was a woman's lively voice singing to the Mohammedans. With the exception of his fingers, which suited a piano teacher, there was nothing about Qasim the Rooster that matched that voice.

Davenport listened while the Rooster plunged into his traditional prologue for a quarter hour. We had all memorized that prologue by heart from the many times it had floated through the early-afternoon air: "God preserve our sultan! The imam of sultans, the possessor of emperors and kings, the guarantor and bestower of crowns upon all the kings of the world. God keep him happy with blessings upon the land, the successful one, the defender, capable and triumphant, and absolute master of the Black Sea and the White Mediterranean; of Rumelia, Anatolia, Karaman, of the lands of the Byzantines and the Copts, of Kurdistan, Azerbaijan, and Turkmenistan, of the Persian lands, of Damascus and Aleppo, of Cairo, of Mecca, of Enlightened Medina, of Jerusalem, of all the Arab lands, of Yemen, of all the inhabited regions conquered by his noble ancestors and magnificent forebears—may God shine upon their tombs . . ."

Because the Rooster had been engrossed in two earthquakes that had occurred the previous Thursday, he did not much care about the alarming events that had happened on the Shatt in recent days, and he did not come to mention them except in the very end of his sermon. Earthquakes were his favorite topic, so much so that, if none had taken place, the people said he would invent one in his imagination so as to preach to the people about it. That day he was eagerly describing the latest earthquake. The words of his sermon were saturated with utter pleasure. He spoke as though he were churning butter. Describing the earth tremor, he said it was a "veritable chastisement," and it was not for him to ward it off us. Verily, God makes His signs clear to us. He sends us warnings and admonitions so that we may stop and make a reckoning, and to censure and punish ourselves before the universal castigation, when the angel Gabriel places his wing under the city and overturns it, just as fields are plowed to expose the soil to the sun, just as happened to the people of Lot. Or else he sends deadly birds from heaven to bombard us with stones, as happened to the Abyssinian general mentioned in the Qur'an.

In the second part of the sermon, the Rooster requested mercy for my father. I didn't realize that a prayer for mercy meant that the one being prayed for was counted among the dead. Having decided that my father was dead, the Rooster had free rein to tell stories and anecdotes about him. He recounted luminous moments that brought the two of them together in the throng of boats, or on a bench in the vegetable-sellers market, or in the funeral processions of the great and mighty, which my father so often walked behind, delivering eulogies to pay respects to the deceased. "He was a Christian, but he was charitable. God Almighty says in His book: 'Indeed, whoever submits his face to God and is charitable shall have a reward with his Lord.' Hear the word of God, brothers! 'Whoever submits . . . and is charitable': this means that Father Emmo was a Mohammedan without realizing it." The Rooster stopped to give the people a moment to marvel. Then he continued. "He was the best person I've ever met. The image of his ghost, which emerged before me yesterday, remains before my eyes. As I finished washing my feet in the fountain and was about to proceed to the mihrab, I saw him before me. His face shone with beauty, casting a green light. He whispered a few words in my ear, and then I heard the rustle of his wings as they struck the ground before Father Emmanuel flew into the sky, bidding me farewell and pointing his finger at me as though reminding me of the words he had whispered. God have mercy upon you, O faithful servant!"

The Rooster had spent the previous five years cursing my father and advising people not to shake hands with him. What had happened, and why had he reversed his stance so quickly? During my time in that city,

I had seen the Rooster turn inside out and change his views and ways of thinking time after time.

"Maybe he learned how to preach from the Zurkhaneh," said Baghdadli.

The Zurkhaneh was a form of martial arts he had been famous for before the sultan had promoted him to preacher of the province. The people had not forgotten the Rooster's former title, the Zurkhaneh Lion, even after he exchanged the wrestler's headband for a turban. The widespread story of a Zurkhaneh fighter being raised to the province's pulpit was known to all. The Rooster had a brother who was famous for administering sharia schools and who issued fatwas in his spare time. One of his fatwas helped establish the sultan's rule in Istanbul. The fatwa spoke of the permissibility of killing the sultan's siblings in order to prevent the disorder that would come if they tried to rival him for the throne. As a result, this brother of Qasim the Rooster, Asim, who was fierce as a rooster himself, achieved all his requests and desires, while Qasim became preacher of Basra and the lands under its domain in the Arabian Gulf.

FATUHA'S PROCESSION AND THE SHIRT MADE OF WATER

After the prayers were finished, it was clear that Sheikh Qasim the Rooster, the Zurkhaneh Lion, the Imam of the Qawnaq, skilled in his words regarding the Kadhim of the province, was not the only one to whom my father had appeared in those days. All those who passed by the hospital after the sheikh's sermon mentioned my father's appearance to them or to their relatives somewhere. The next day, Khando came to us to greet his sister, kiss her head, and give her one hundred qirsh, as he always did. He said he took in three times that amount from selling songs to churches, taverns, and the tribal theaters of the Mohammedans. He informed us that people had gathered at the palm tree field because the dates were ripe for harvesting, and they claimed that the priest had been observed resting at the top of a palm tree. He'd been tucked up there with a leg in his hand. The sight of him was terrifying at first, looking exactly as though he had torn off the leg of his opponent in a bloody battle, especially since the people of those parts had rarely seen an artificial leg. People said the same green light that the Rooster had mentioned during prayers soon appeared from his face and began reflecting onto the faces of the peasants and the date harvester. The vision of Father Emmo beamed with kindness and nobility, which made people begin to feel distressed at his disappearance. People rushed barefoot, carrying their naked children, to seek a blessing from his light. Even though he remained there for only a few moments, he began taking them by surprise and appearing in their homes, which they left nearly empty. He was observed among the housewives and in frying pans, waterspouts, the bottoms of skillets, and water pouring out of pitchers.

On the following day, in the early-morning hours, Rahlo's son, Janah, came and repeated the same story as Khando, adding a tale that filled us with excitement and made Baghdadli pick me up and rush me to the shore. The son of the blind prostitute, who was only a few months older than me, informed us that he had seized the man from the Overleaf Society who had vowed to shake my father's hand and drink water from the same cup. He had captured him while he was lying at the wall of the mosque of Fatuha Umm al-Aqdar. The members of the Overleaf Society would often wait for human gatherings like this to slip in, encounter rivals, and pose slick, dogmatic questions, which could never be grasped or put to rest. Most often, they ended in some logical fallacy or intellectual dead end, like the example of the chicken or the egg, which no one in this city has yet been able to determine which came first.

Janah dragged him from his circle and led him like an Eid sheep destined for slaughter to his kuphar, a round boat used by young people such as Janah to get around on the river or to gather late into the night in the dry summer. He brought the man to Quarantine Island, which is a spot of dry land in the heart of the Shatt. Soldiers have built a wall there of reed stalks and baked mud, in the center of which is an enormous tent erected upon a metal base. Sick people and travelers coming from every direction are crammed into that tent on that island, which the Qawnaq uses as a quarantine site to protect the city from sickness and plague. There, new arrivals are examined assiduously in order to confirm they are safe from any contagious diseases. Janah tied the neck to his belt and then wrapped the rest of the rope around his face. He didn't intend to bring him inside the quarantine tent, which was well guarded by soldiers from the Ninth Armed Regiment, but instead, he knew of a hidden room under a dirt hillock behind the watchtower standing at one end of the island where no one ever went. He put the man there and hurried to the tavern where Khando was singing in order to inform him of what he had acquired.

Khando took us to Quarantine Island in the company of Janah. The plan was for us to meet the man without Davenport catching wind of our activities. My anxiety had penetrated Baghdadli's heart, and she adopted my views, no longer trusting the assistant deputy vice consul. Not far from there, it happened that people were carrying out the wali's orders to hunt down stray dogs, which were commonly known to carry ticks, lap water from mosque washing fountains, and dig up tomato patches and banana bunches. So the people had gathered whatever dirty, wet dogs they could manage, some with hides disfigured and scarred from beatings. They put all the dogs in rice sacks, ignoring the animals' terror as they swung and jumped about inside the bags. Then they shot them in order to silence the bags. The bags became still and trickled streams of blood. All our necks turned as we rode Janah's kuphar away from the dogs' slaughterhouse, catching the last howl as it died away.

"Someone get me out of the big rice sack that I'm living in," murmured Shathra.

We entered the room that Janah had sprinkled with water, causing the smell of mud to rise and produce a sense of numbness. It combined with the smell of the night lily to make me yawn. The prisoner was stretched out on his belly, writing on a stack of papers he had spread around him. His face had the imprints of lines, on account of the rope that had been wrapped around it. The man was not afraid, nor did he show any sign that he had been kidnapped only a short time before. He asked for tea, which Rahlo's son brought to him and left him blowing over it.

"Come with me," said Janah, taking Khando's hand and pulling him aside some meters from the entrance to the dirt room. "Let's leave the guarded one with the nuns." Perhaps they lit up a hookah there and began talking about the normal things that men talk about. By *guarded one*, he meant the prisoner from the Overleaf Society, and by *the nuns*, he meant Baghdadli and me! Baghdadli bent to the ear of her brother and whispered, "Tell Rahlo's son I'm no longer considered a nun."

The man was calm and dignified despite his caricatured appearance, lying on his belly and waving his feet in the air. He drew the polluted air into his nose and produced a disgusting whistle as he snorted the snot up his nostrils. Previously, Janah had described this man as someone who "talks out of his ass." I wondered whether we might possibly observe that. Then I realized that they meant his pompous manner of speaking, which was of no consequence to anyone. Some time passed after our entrance into the room where he had been impounded. He kept hanging his head and tracing his thumb over the words written on the back of the papers scattered around him. He avoided meeting my eye or Baghdadli's. When he became aware of our presence, he bowed his head even closer to the ground as a way to show us an even greater degree of respect.

"People have magnified my story, but it's only a small thing," said the man, whose original name turned out to be Salman, though he was known among the people as Ring Finger. He went on: "It's true that I vowed to drink from the cup of the priest, but I swear to you, by any priest or imam you wish . . ." He paused to lick his lips. "I swear to you—choose the lord or god or priest that is appropriate for me to swear by—that I haven't come across Father Emmo for the past month." A suffocating odor of date wine emanated from his mouth with each syllable he pronounced, and the only thing that saved us was the letter *M,* when he closed his mouth to articulate it and confined the fermented-date vapors. When he realized we did not wish to hurt him, he loosed the reins of his ponderous tongue, which made a racket of jumbled words. He brought his face closer to my lower half and rubbed his eyes to make sure he was seeing a child with her leg cut off, but the sight did not help him fashion a clear sentence. He began singing the songs that invaded him and did allow his throat a moment's rest. Meanwhile, Baghdadli, whose smiles were infectious, smiled as she saw the writings tattooed on his forearm. At that time, reading Arabic was not as easy for me as it is now, especially when it wasn't written clearly on paper. The man did not resist as Baghdadli pulled his arm over so that his whole forearm was between her hands. From his arm, she read to me texts from the Qur'an, the Gospels, and the Old Testament. Our skin crawled for a few seconds, and then both of us leaned back against the wall, laughing.

From his shoulder down to his wrist was a line of green words that spoke a verse from the Bible: "The Lord God is my strength: He makes my feet like a gazelle and helps me mount the high places, and don't squeeze my burning armpit with your hot fingers." Baghdadli asked me what the second line meant as a way to test my intelligence, as she often did. I answered that it seemed likely that he had gotten that tattoo at Rahlo's brothel, and that he cried out to the prostitute giving him the tattoo not to come near his armpit, which was on fire due to the sweat and the heat.

"I once asked Father Emmo to choose a verse from the Bible for me to write on my forearm," said Ring Finger. "I wanted to add it to my skin, right next to a verse from the Qur'an, but my companion at Rahlo's place, who was good at writing and giving tattoos and biting, did not listen well to what I told her. She had abandoned her writing exercises, and she was no longer up to the exercises I gave her. She was drunk, and when I was groaning in pain, she added my angry words to the tattoo."

On the way back, the kuphar was not big enough for the five of us. Baghdadli rode with her brother, and I rode with Janah and Ring Finger aboard a second kuphar. Janah connected the boats with a piece of rope and kept calling to me that I stop leaning over the side to study my face in the water, as I always liked to do. People's faces look older in the water, as my father used to say, not because the water infuses them with extra years, but because the river shows a girl her father's face instead of the reflection of her own. When he was still here, my father would play that trick on me. He would gently push my face down toward the water and then cover one of my eyes with his palm and look down from behind me at the surface of the water, making me see him as though his face were my face.

"I'll get out at the Abu Kishra rocket," said Ring Finger. Janah didn't stop him, but he bent toward us a little in order to release his drunken prisoner, who had not stopped singing and raving and reciting proverbs, verses of poetry, and the names of anchored ships, using many rough and antiquated words. Khando bent his ear to listen in from where he rode behind us in the kuphar with his sister. They did not want to miss a single word that Ring Finger uttered.

"Look, before I get off at the rocket: there's something fishy about this business of Father Emmo. How can a man go missing in these parts when he's British, red-haired, and white like an albino? When he's under the protection of the Crown . . . and the cross, and the lily, and the crescent, and the feather? Don't blame me. He is a beloved man. I saw him with my own eyes when, on a single day, he circumcised fifty boys. He did everything, and he did not scorn even to clean the noses of beggars, the pock-marked, the outcasts, and the insane. Perhaps you know that I am Ring Finger, ranked fifth in the Overleaf Society. Do you know why they call us the Gang of Five? It's because we are the only ones who don't want to change anyone's religion or sect in a city where everyone is trying to change everyone else. And because we do not pay taxes and tolls, and we do not believe that foreigners bring the plague with them, hidden in their suitcases. Along those lines, we also wear shoes, we comb our hair, we pass our hours calling upon jars of ink as they recede behind the reed pen." The reed was the pen people used for writing Arabic script. It was made from dry, hard stalks of reed.

"Do you think wine makes me drunk? No! It's the wine of letters spilling over the white page. I don't say this to everybody, but you don't seem like the others. I make it all plain to you. Sometimes I choke when I look at the forms of the letters and their magical swirls. They aren't actually moving, but they do so in my mind. Yes, this sweat blocked all my senses. It did not make me drunk. It blocked my spirit and exchanged it for a chicken's eagerness for flight. I will think of a way to help you tomorrow after having tea and cream. Drop me off here, right here at my grandfather's rocket."

"It's my rocket!" I said.

"I'm sorry, my lady. It's my rocket, rising out of the ground, and I inherited it from my father. My grandfather emigrated from the Levant and came here. He was the sole agent of the sultans for building rockets. Actually, in his entire life, he only designed a single rocket, namely this one—under which, I will now take a piss."

The Persian Empire had readied itself for war and gathered its material and armies on the eastern edge of the city, a position they held for many days. "It was a tedious threat and a foolish verbal war. If only they had fought it out and relieved us of the people and relieved the people of us and of themselves! In the beginning, it was merely a war of pulpits, books, and poems. Many diverse creeds sprang up to divide the two Mohammedan camps on its account. Then, when things became serious, they asked my grandfather to design a rocket that they erected on the Shatt. A long-distance rocket that would not disintegrate or melt before prostrating itself upon its target. All prior attempts to create military rockets had died in their places before even getting a start. Rockets crashed before launching, and in the best-case scenario, the engineer and his interpreter would be thrown in prison. But my grandfather was executed! It was because he had spent two years in charge of his scraps and all the provisions, raw materials, and metals that the weapons team provided him. His weight dropped by half. He was a Hercules, striding like an elephant, but then he could not rise from his bed without the help of his servant. When the day dawned for inaugurating the rocket, the wali attended as the sultan's representative. A not-insignificant number of officials attended in order to test the rocket before its announcement, and the people gathered for a joyous celebration. But the rocket did not launch. It fell back to the earth, plowed a trench, and stuck there. And if only that were all! Instead, it emitted a poisonous gas that did not affect the entire body but only the face. People's faces tightened and stretched from the pain and the clotting blood. But their mouths were bared in a smile, or sometimes even a laugh. That is why it was subsequently called "the disease of Abu Kishra," or "Mr. Hilarity." Those days were a significant trial for everyone because they never got a rest from burying their dead killed by the plague. At the same time, they found themselves hurling smiles at each other for no reason, unable to control their faces. Boisterous laughter passed involuntarily between them. It made them like fools who care about nothing, even though they are filled with disappointments, bereavements, and the loss of loved ones. Only the person afflicted by the bizarre rocket gas knew that he was crying and not laughing, contrary to what other people thought. It was a gas from out of this world, and whoever made it was, without a doubt, a brilliant scholar who had emerged from some demonic realm. That would be my grandfather, may he rest in peace, who also died with a grimace before they were able to execute him so that he did not meet his death as a punishment. Actually, most of the people who were afflicted by that illness died without anyone knowing that they were in pain. Instead, people thought they were dying from laughter. They were cursed by the state mufti of that time, who exhorted them, saying that much laughter kills the heart, but he did not know they had lost control of their faces. If they were able to drive that bitter laughter from their mouths, they would have torn the flesh of the mufti's face and gnawed on his bones. There is nothing harder than the pain that people envy."

Ring Finger got out of the kuphar, half his leg sinking into the mud. He was heavy, and getting out required a patience we did not possess. Janah struck him on the collar, giving him a push so that he fell flat on his face. He rolled over so he could sit his corpse-like body up as he screamed, "You son of a blind whore! A slut who feels and hears but never sees the man between her legs! You slipped out of a public pussy packed with algae and catfish!" He stood up, and a column of blood trickled down his belly. He wasn't upset, and there wasn't any trace of anger on his face, even as he cursed so loudly with vulgarities that insulted the house of Janah's mother.

"Tell me, you son of the pussy palace, you bastard of the rotting boats—who told you she was your mother? For all you know, maybe she traded you for some other whoreson. Who knows?" After that, he was content to keep laughing while he related some unimportant story as we drifted away. "Do you know how the rocket stopped making people laugh?" His voice was still reaching us with all its rattling and coughing. "After only three days, when the contagion of explosive laughter had infected even the nursing infants, a man proposed that the people study their fingernails. Or that they lift their hands and look at their fingertips. That was actually enough to fix the laughing mouths and lock them up before it was too late and they died. And that is what happened. Their mouths shriveled up and puckered shut like a purse of dirhams. No! Like a chicken's asshole! And that plague was lifted from us forever, even if we did not need to be freed entirely from laughter. We would have been happy to keep a little of it."

Baghdadli whispered to me that he was referring to the rumor that says that when a person looks at his fingertips, he will inevitably remember the paradise he was kicked out of, and he will feel ashamed of himself. "Disgrace and laughter cannot coexist," said Baghdadli. "Adam did not have fingernails when he was in paradise, so looking closely at our fingertips pushes our minds back to the distant past when we were still sperm in his loins. We feel grief on those days of utter happiness. Shame oozes from every pore of our bodies, and we feel wretched and sad."

"I remembered something!" Ring Finger was still raving as Janah tried to maneuver the two kuphar boats and row them over to the quay across from Strangers Hospital. "Have you forgotten the guide to the lost on Quarantine Island? That woman who is as divided as though she were the train to Kazakhstan: Did you forget her, or did she run away? This is the last kuphar that will cross over today. She'll have to wait until next week. She'll die of hunger, or something bad might happen to her."

Baghdadli struck her forehead, and the others shook at the thought. I was not concerned by Shathra's presence or absence. Her scent had expanded over the past two days and become like an ostrich running on ahead of her. In the past two days, she had been less attentive to the matter of my leg and my father. From the bulge of her bag, which she wore on her chest like a middle breast, it seemed she had acquired some money from selling otter puppies to foreigners. I had not witnessed that myself yet, but the secret of that trade of hers was in the mouths of patients that day. Perhaps that explained the set of her face recently and her swaggering gait. From where we were, I could see her standing on the bank of Quarantine Island and raising her hand. I told everyone it was Shathra, waving at us.

"What is that she's holding?" asked Khando.

"It's the statue of Baby Jesus!"

It appeared that Shathra had stumbled across my statue on the island and had lifted it up to gesture at us with it. Nevertheless, everyone ignored her. Perhaps she would have to wait until the coming week, as Ring Finger said.

"And another thing before I disappear from your sight," said Ring Finger. "Don't go looking for Father Emmo in the hospitals, police stations, and prisons. Don't waste your time! If he disappeared for some reason of his own, he'll come back for a reason of his own. Otherwise, look for him in the writing of the Overleaf Society."

Because the writing exercises of the Overleaf Society consisted of recording events and meaningless scribbles and word fragments, the important thing was to control the shape of the letters, not the content of the writing. It often happened that their pens took what was going on around them and dragged it to the page. Ring Finger compared that process to the twisting and pulling of a carpet thread so that the carpet grew thin and weak. They pulled on the events and all the words that flew around them. An addiction to writing demands that—a love for the intoxication of writing, not for the sake of recording.

"I know some of the Overleaf Society have brains you could swap with a mule's bladder," Ring Finger continued. "We do not need to understand what we write. You find that one of us might not know what a word means, but he is enchanted by its form and the proportions of its edges and endings. Yes, our endings. They resemble a dagger, an eyebrow, the fold of a lovely woman's belly when she sits and tilts her thighs like flippers." He cleared his throat as he said that, suddenly remembering that two women were present in the kuphar boats. That didn't bother us, since we were focused on what he was saying.

It seemed as though Khando was the one who had let go of his oar and released it from its oarlock. I heard him say to his sister, "Maybe we will know from their papers where my hat has disappeared to."

"Yes, I pray to God that we will find that old hat of yours quickly," Baghdadli replied. "We forgot your mind in it, and you've been missing it ever since that day."

Khando, who did not ignore his sister's mockery of him, wanted to say something to prove his mind was still with him and hadn't been lost along with his hat. "There are big things happening around here, and they are usually covered up by other things like the disappearance of Father Emmo or the discovery of a girl's headless body . . . All those things that people concoct are like sheets and blankets to cover some big event they don't want the people to notice. On the day that Father Emmo disappeared, my friends and I observed a big nose walking in the river. Then we noticed that the nose was erected on a boat being rowed by tribesmen who were being guarded by slaves of the sheikhs. Then, in another boat, we saw two stone ears a little longer than that nose. After that, we saw a black eye covered in garlic boxes on one of the river convoys. An enormous cranium bigger than an elephant passed by here. The stone face of King Hammurabi, pushed by the English and the Germans with the help of sheikhs. They took it there. They wanted to mesmerize people with a fleet belonging to the king of bygone centuries. Do you know why? I think they were concealing the procession of Sayyida Fatuha, the sultan's wife, as she passed through here on her way to the pilgrimage, so that the people would not see the lights of her beauty."

Then we laughed in astonishment for Ring Finger had loosened the ties of his pants and dropped them in a sudden motion so that his parts hung down and released his golden faucet, urinating out in the open and in front of our departing eyes. Ring Finger felt embarrassed by the fact of our being embarrassed, so we were even.

We arrived. Janah struck his kuphar and, with a final blow, brought us close to the door of the hospital. Khando and his sister were still making light of Ring Finger's words and joking among themselves. After we reached the entrance, Janah remained in his kuphar, wiping his head and his chest, as though cleaning them of imaginary blood that had flowed after a savage fight. I turned my head and kept my eyes on his face as I walked along, but he did not move from his place. Then I was distracted by a commotion caused by a Sind sparrow as it shook out its nest in the palm tree. I heard the splash of the water coming from Janah plunging loudly into the Shatt. "He'll come out on the other side of the river," I remarked to Baghdadli. "Janah considers the river to be his shirt. When he was small, Rahlo sewed him a shirt using fabric she gathered from the flags stolen off of ships. Every day, she kept pulling on his limbs, and every day, the shirt got bigger. That did not prevent her from presenting him with the shirt. As soon as he saw it, he was overcome with fury and struck his head against the wall. He tore the shirt and bewailed his lot in life. As for Rahlo, she was angry at that behavior of his. She snatched the shirt back from him and threw it into the river. So the entire river became his shirt."

THE THIRD QUARTER

ISABELLA'S EYES

Atop his mule, Davenport was waiting for us at the door of the hospital, the midday sun beating down upon them both. As we approached, his animal released the reins on its bladder, stirring up a cloud of dust that obscured Davenport entirely from sight and reached all the way to his yellow turban. We tried to elude him and made a beeline for the hospital gate, but he beat us there and stood in our path. Davenport hopped to the ground. His turban slid to the side, revealing how unaccustomed it was to sitting upon his skull. On certain occasions, particularly Mohammedan events, the assistant deputy vice consul wore a thick turban that resembled a spongy cake. That helped spread a rumor, which he himself had planted, that he was converting to their religion. The result was that some judges, sons of pashas, date merchants, and brokers would besiege him with questions at their parties. His weary voice and his confusion would come to his aid when he denied his conversion decisively, succeeding at appearing afraid of revealing the matter of his conversion but leaving it to the Holy King. They would keep quiet about his news and show their affection, which granted him a feeling of crafty satisfaction. "We know you've converted to our religion," they'd say, "but you're afraid of your subordinates." At that, Davenport would smile, ease spreading over his features, and he would strike a deal for wool and goat hair, which would guarantee his joy for weeks to come. A joy that would reflect upon the entire Strangers Hospital since he often volunteered to repair something or supply us with additional beds or a new washbasin, or he would pay the deferred debts of the Gospel sellers whom we hired and who came back to us at the end of the day without having sold a single book.

As we passed him, he avoided, as he did every time, directing his gaze at Baghdadli, who always enjoyed tormenting him by staring directly into his face, which increased his confusion and his sweat. One time, I heard him exclaim to my father, "When will your nuns stop biting, O Father?" referring to what I called "the Day of the Bite." That was the day when Baghdadli took a fair-size bite out of his dignity. She did not approach him with her teeth but reached out with her words, which snapped like invisible fangs, deadly as poison. He kept stomping the ground like a child bursting into a temper tantrum after his parents stopped him from picking his nose. It happened one day when he came into the room as my father had his fingers deep inside the mouth of an elderly patient in an attempt to ease his pain. Davenport was drunk, which meant he would be mocking everyone and everything. I was behind Baghdadli, watching the face of the patient. He said to me, "And how's our patron saint of girls with orphaned shoes?" He was referring to the fact that whenever we bought shoes that fit my artificial right leg, we also had to buy the left shoe of the pair. And when we bought shoes for my real left foot, we had to buy the right shoe. I kept storing up the other shoe of the pair until I had a big sack filled with brand-new shoes that had never been worn. When I heard him say *orphaned shoes*, I couldn't contain my laughter, which exploded through the room. The assistant deputy vice consul would have possessed a good sense of humor had he focused a bit more on his words. My mind had not yet finished digesting his sentence, and at first I thought he was praising me. Then I realized he was making fun of me. My cheeks began burning, and I felt hurt inside, just like I always did. That's when Baghdadli raised her head and took a step back, which is what she usually did when she wanted to sting someone. "Welcome, Davenport," she said. "God bless you! The assistant deputy vice consul of hollow eyes has arrived!" He grabbed a cup of water and gulped it down in one drink, trying to hydrate his skin, which was being dried out by the alcohol. His lower lip dangled down, and water dribbled out of his mouth onto his beard and the tail of his turban, which he had thrown over his shoulder.

By *hollow eyes*, she was referring to his old profession of plucking small bits out of gold coins and selling them. I only knew foggy patches of that story, picked up here and there. The gist of it was that Davenport had been accused of plucking out the eyes of the portrait of Queen Isabella's face found on gold coins. He would then melt down those tiny bits and fragments and sell them. In those days, the Treasury Department issued golden coins bearing the image of the queen of Spain to celebrate her visit to the American West Coast. Davenport was subsequently thrown in prison after an allegation was made that he was carving into the queen's face and extracting specks of gold, which he then sold to jewelers after melting down the gold pieces and forming them into ingots the size of a matchbox. He decided to carve out a spot from the heart of the coin instead of the edge, which had a fringe of notched teeth. Focusing on the face of the queen, he used a fine chisel to drill out the lump depicting her eyes and eyelids, also taking a bite of her wrinkled cheek on rare occasions. It was an excellent choice, given that people looking at the coins did not inspect the faces of kings and emperors on the coins so much as they cared deeply about the notched edge. The impetus for the charge was that a widow mother from the indigenous tribes complained that her son was afraid of hard currency. He would become terrified, screaming and crying, if she placed a coin in his hand or his eye ever fell upon one. It seems that one of the coins Davenport had bored into had come to that mother, and the queen's face had terrified her child because parts of her eyes and lips had been removed. News of the allegation spread throughout the city, and a dozen lawyers stepped forward to defend the mother. That led to

Davenport's first downfall, and he lost bits of his laudable reputation and his psychological resilience against slanderous calumny.

Perhaps he gained half his wealth from Isabella's eyes. The truth was, according to my father's testimony, that Davenport renounced that first craft of his and immigrated to Arabia, where he would buy cotton, keep the pashas company, and pretend he was an ashamed Mohammedan who hid his religion to avoid being censured by his government. Yet all that did not succeed in removing the story of the hollow eyes from Baghdadli's tongue and the memory of Father Emmo.

After getting down from his mule, Davenport struck it on the haunch and sent it hurrying away from us. Baghdadli led me away and bent her head to release one side of the gate. Davenport beat her to it and opened the gate through its viewing window. She ignored his actions and proceeded toward the hall. When we went inside, we learned the reason Davenport was waiting for us at the gate. His guards trained in rumors had told him that we had left on some errand related to my father, which made him appear less driven and eager to demonstrate his good intentions and continue the search for him. He repeated the same words that he did every time, about the city not being safe and that true safety lie only in leaving the matter to the Qawnaq police, who knew how to pull the threads of this city and sift them through their fingers like water in a cup. But he emphasized this time that the consequences would be severe if we repeated that deed of ours.

"I was attracted to the Overleaf Society before you were. Curiosity drove me to learn what their writing exercises contained. Like you, I believed they were recording events automatically for the sake of practicing calligraphy and making their writing ever more beautiful. I wished to get to know the history of our Evangelicalism here after the consul asked the vice consul for a report on that topic. The vice consul asked his deputy, who approached me in my capacity as his assistant. I completed the report and was about to deliver it to him, but my constant perfectionism complex pushed me to continue searching and asking in order to add some simple touches to the report. I heard about the Overleaf Society and sought them out. After two months of searching for them, they were still playing a game of cat and mouse with me—or cat and mouse and bullfrog! It was no easy matter to get my hands on those weasels. One of them was called Ibham, which means *Thumb*. He was fat and had dark skin, sunken eyes, and a face half-eaten by scabies. I paid him sixty lira to open for me the old exercises written by his teachers and his teachers' teachers. You know that this society is very old. Every one of them entrusts his charge to someone new before dying. Thumb demonstrated a churlish manner towards me. I did not come across anything that caught my eye. I won't deny that the script was the height of magnificence, and that looking at it was an intoxicating, stupefying pleasure. But taken together, it was just isolated letters and scribbles that did not amount to anything other than a demonstration of the precise formation of letters and how to join them together. I found nothing of value in them. They recorded the first days of our mission and trivial things such as the storks that landed on the roofs, the elephant that entered the city as a gift from the Persian sultan to the Turkish sultan. It did not appear that they often busied themselves with writing history and its everyday events. If their pages contain anything besides descriptions of the weather and birds and beasts and scattered words, I would be the first to seek their help in learning your father's fate. Don't waste our time and get us in trouble with the wali!"

Baghdadli went up to my room, just as she always did after the assistant deputy vice consul withdrew. She explained his words to me and what lay hidden behind them, as though they were cryptic occult texts. She believed that Davenport longed to strike a deal with a high-ranking official close to the wali that would allow him to buy the Tides Office so that he would have a share in the profits from the office responsible for promulgating the tide schedules to ships, consulates, and river barges. All of that required that he first win the trust of all parties to the deal, using gifts and presents to wipe away a past associated with bits of golden coins gouged from the faces of kings and emperors. There is no greater advantage than the possession of time. The schedules of the water rising and falling among the thickets and trunks, the schedules for the opening of the canals and passages. It meant writing the timetables and selling them, written and confirmed, finishing business in time and gaining the days to come. This was a difficult deal, given that membership in the office at that time belonged to the family of the sheikhs whose synagogue overlooked the Shatt and who possessed most of the businesses, the gardens, and the modern German ships on the river.

Before Baghdadli went back down, I asked her where we could find the Overleaf Society. She objected by placing her hand on my forehead and pressing my head into my pillow. "Listen: let's go out together and ask the people about the events that occurred on the day your father disappeared. Cooperating with the Overleaf Society will bring us troubles that will only be followed by further reckless actions from your uncle." Sometimes, and without correcting herself, Baghdadli called Davenport my uncle. It appeared that she was beginning to dread him and was retreating from her earlier zeal. "Ever since my transfer to Basra, news about that society of scribes has not stopped boring into my head. Last time, they attacked the Qawnaq's shipbuilder and hired the dregs of the earth, the misfortunate, and the little sheikhs to help them liberate their ship, which the wali had confiscated. In that ship are ancient writing exercises that go back hundreds of years. There is another problem, which is that most young people here claim to belong to the Overleaf Society. Your father says that the society consists of just five scribes, no more, but they are not known, and they conceal their identities, revealing themselves only to those they trust. I myself have treated more than six individuals who claimed to be part of the Overleaf Society. Sleep, my dear, sleep!"

That day did not end before Shathra knocked on my door with the statue of Baby Jesus under her arm. Her face, and the halo of happiness radiating from it, made me feel a general sense of joy. That made me realize how much I had missed her, even though she had only been gone for a matter of hours. She brought me down to the hall where Baghdadli was sitting with her patient. Around us was a calm that swept the place with a brief pause in the snoring, as though the dozens of patients hidden under the sheets were presenting us with a gift. Shathra sat at the foot of the bed, and I peppered her with questions. "Where did you find the statue? How did you get it back, Shathra?" It seemed a stupid question to pose to a registered guide to the lost, but through this short time with her, I came to believe that, in her current condition, she was not as strong as she appeared to be or as she used to appear.

"I took it away from a boy who was carrying it as he walked along, followed by six fishermen."

According to her description of the boy, there was no doubt in my mind who it was, and I spoke his name aloud to her: "Finjan."

The compact boy who had been my companion in my failed attempt to run away.

Finjan had acquired Baby Jesus on his way. I'm not able to determine how. Perhaps he'd followed me after I got out of his boat and wandered along the shore around the building that looked like Strangers Hospital. Shathra told me that he fought back hard to keep her from taking the statue away. He wanted it to accompany him wherever the fishermen were taking him.

"Where were the fishermen taking him, Shathra?" I asked.

"They were taking him to the river ring," she said.

"And where's the river ring, Shathra?" I asked. I fell silent after my question.

She bit her right wrist. "The ring is not a place," she said, "and no one goes there." She said it with a kind of embarrassment while making gestures with her fingers. She made a ring with one hand, thrusting the index finger of her other hand in and out with a jerking motion. I understood that the fishermen had used Finjan for their pleasure.

It appeared that the men of the Shatt were used to using the softness of his body to find a release by discharging their animals inside his boyhood. They took turns with Finjan, and he did not resist them. Perhaps he received certain benefits from them, such as permission to row among them and claim skill and standing among his relatives and in the eyes of his mother, who questioned him and watched him and wanted him to enjoy life and his work on the river. When he came home each day, she would plumb his memory, asking him about everything and recounting his exploits to her neighbors. Perhaps on one of those same occasions, as she smiled with pride over her son, the milk of the fishermen's loins was dripping down his legs as he related what people said about his skill and how they did not subject him to any biting criticism of his youthful abilities. As for our statue, he wanted to keep that wooden doll to play with while they were drinking their harmful things—or at least, so he would not have to cry alone. For the doll, with its sad face filled with innocence, would cry with him. I'm not sure whom that statue actually represented at that time in the mind of Finjan: the Jesus I knew or the grandson of the Prophet Mohammed. But I am certain that the statue and the Lord of the statue were looking down on him at that time to comfort him and distract him from the pain.

"And how did you get back here, Shathra?"

"Father Emmo," said Shathra as she threaded a needle and used it to mend a tear on one of her sleeves.

"This is no time for jokes," said Baghdadli.

"The boat of Father Emmo is the one that delivered me here. I was sleeping on the Shatt. The wind uncovered my belly, and the Chinese steamship workers laughed at my big belly button. One of them threw a coconut shell at me and indicated I should cover my belly button with it, as though it were a pot lid. At that moment, I heard a boat colliding with the bank. It was the decorated boat of Father Emmo. I heard him ask me to get in, so I got in. The boat began moving on its own and brought me back to Strangers Hospital. I got out of the boat so it could head off towards the heart of the One-Eyed Tigris."

"Shathra, I want you to clean these catfish with me. Come along!" Baghdadli called out to her to take her away from me and put an end to her inappropriate joke. The catfish that Khando had purchased were hanging in a net, guarded by the eyes of the patients, whose mouths were running with their appetite.

Shathra got up and went with her. Baghdadli grabbed her forearm and pinched it, silently reprimanding her. Meanwhile, Shathra shook her head to deny it was a joke. She swore to God that it really was Father Emmo's boat that had delivered her there. She let him know plainly that after he was gone, the hospital had gone to ruin. Sick strangers came into it, and they went out again, still sick and sad. No one believed Shathra. What she said about the past and present was worthy of the trash heap. Everyone agreed, including Khando and Madelena, that Shathra was playing with my mind and ought not to be believed.

THE POPE OF THE MARSH ARABS

For me, the most beautiful thing in the Arabic language was the shadda. I used to think that people wrote it in as a decoration, and I imagined it as a butterfly landing on the words. I put one on all my words. Then, when I learned that it was placed only over the consonant that was doubled, I used it less and replaced it with a drawing of a small ladybug, without the black spots on its shell. When I first saw the texts of the Overleaf Society, I saw so many shaddas that they appeared to be a whole swarm of ladybugs swimming among the words. As for how I first came across the texts of the Overleaf Society, that is the story I will relate next.

Right at midnight, Davenport opened the door to my room. I was surprised and frightened. Whenever Davenport passed through the door to my room, I was unable to look at his face, for the sight of him always filled me with disgust. He always directed his gaze at my chest, not at my face. When he entered my room that night, I thought he had in mind to carry out some deed with my body.

I do not deny that I exaggerated in showing the fear on my face. But I was not exaggerating when I wet myself. That happened spontaneously, even to the point that I got his hand wet, which was leaning on my bed. He shouted at me twice to be silent, even though I was already quiet. He went on calmly, turning his face away from me. He took out his long notebook from behind him and spread it out before me.

"Now, just be quiet like the crazy girls. Don't tell anyone what I'm about to show you, not even that lazy Arabic nun."

Baghdadli was not lazy, of course. Davenport just thought that everyone here was lazy and negligent.

Davenport opened his notebook. He began smoothing one page after another until he found it—a normal page, slightly greenish. I didn't need him to say that it was from the Overleaf Society; I guessed that right away. He brought the page close to my face, and I read it with difficulty. It appeared to be a receipt for a quantity of calves between the Portuguese consulate and a Mohammedan butcher. On the back were the writing exercises of the Overleaf Society. But the calligraphic writings did not overwhelm me like people say. It was beautiful and fascinating, without a doubt, but I did not tremble or melt from desire. Perhaps fear had disabled my senses.

"This is the page that I bought from Thumb. He did not write it himself. When this page was written, he was only two months old. He brought it to me from the cargo hold of a ship belonging to the Overleaf Society, where they preserve the archives of the former members. Whoever scribed this page was listening to two men, one of whom was a police officer in the Qawnaq during the governorship of Hasram Pasha, thirty years ago, or a little less. From their chatter, he fashioned these lines, written in a rare script. No one before or since has ever written in this style. It took me two weeks before I found someone who could even read it to me. I went around to many individuals. You know that I read and write Arabic better than you and your father, but these lines gave me a headache."

I asked him to close the door and help me move from the bed to the floor. That pleased him, and it made him see that I was as eager as he to learn the secret he was bringing. I allowed myself to take the page between my hands and set it on the bed. He began pointing out the letters and explaining them as he slowly read them to me.

"The officer says that Sister Emma—he means Emma Brown from our Evangelical Mission, and he is speaking, of course, before the founding of this hospital—Sister Emma converted from our church to the Arabic Nestorian Church, and she decided to enter holy orders as a nun. She left the Evangelical Church and all her duties there and set off in her boat, heading for the lakes. She lived there for a time among the tribes of the Marsh Arabs, spending perhaps ten years there. She turned her boat into a church. She did not preach or try to convert anyone. Instead, she devoted herself to worshipping God, and she tied her hair to the prow of her boat at night so that her fatigue would not catch up to her and prevent her from praising God even for a moment. She decided to go further and live among the Marsh Arabs, but it was hard to do that as a woman on her own. So she decided to wear a man's clothing and conceal her gender from them entirely. In this way, Sister Emma became the monk Emmanuel, wearing a new name and a man's long robe, and rowing deep into the black waters. He desired—or rather, *she* desired—pure virtue and union with the Lord of Glory, without any blemish. She covered her femininity so that she might present herself to her Lord as a bride, according to her beliefs. Among the Marsh Arabs, she found the quiet, contemplative life she was seeking, pure and innocent. That made the signs and blessings of her Lord come easy to her, until she herself began conferring blessings on others. For their part, the Marsh Arabs got used to the monk Emmanuel and called him Emmo for short."

Davenport noticed that my breaths were coming faster and louder, and he asked whether I was okay. I did not reply. He went on explaining the text.

"One day, a lover slept with his beloved, and she became pregnant. He was despicable enough to run away when her belly began to show. This lover was the youngest son of the sheikh of the tribe, and the girl, who wandered about aimlessly and directed her boat nowhere in particular, found herself facing one of two fates, as the bitter reality of the situation goes: either death to wash away the shame or . . . death to wash away the shame. Emmo, bestower of honors and blessings, kept a distant eye over the village, and its animals brought him news of the people there. The name of the village was Umm al-Jurukh. It did not only move, but it sometimes spun around itself like a planet. Events moved quickly, and the news spread. The distraught girl tried to exit this circular motion. She disappeared from her family for days. She rowed in her boat, slapping the water instead of slapping her own cheeks. No one but the doves heard her voice as she cried, 'Where do I go? Where do I go?' But the dove cannot respond like a parrot: 'Where do I go? Where do I go?' Her uncle's knife caught up to her and sliced her wrist. People dragged her from the boat and brought her to the sheikh's guesthouse. Before the eyes of the sheikh's son, they asked her who had made her pregnant. She did not reply. Father Emmo was the one who replied. 'It was I,' he said—that is, Emma said, 'It was I.' And he begged the sheikh not to torment the girl any further. He decided to offer himself as a ransom for the girl. That is to say, she decided to offer herself as a ransom for the girl and a fitting gift to the Lord, hoping it would be acceptable. The sheikh valued Emmo's confession. As a result, he killed neither the girl nor him, but ordered only that they be banished from the village. They departed it forever. The girl lived with Emmo, who did not reveal to her his truth, never telling her that he was a woman. When the girl gave birth to a daughter, she caught a blood infection, and she died. The daughter lived in the boat of Emma, who is known here today as Father Emmo, and he was father and mother both to the little girl."

As Davenport was relating all this, he sensed my interest in the story, and a smile spread across his face. No doubt he was feeling the triumph of storytellers when their audience rewards them with their full attention. Even though it was a story in a notebook, he was telling it with his fangs, with his nails, and with his hissing. It fell on my head like a shooting star. He cast his words into my memory, through which they delved like an earthworm that became fat as it swallowed everything I knew. He did not need to speak in terms of threat and promise. He did not need to speak anything. I do not remember exactly when he went out, without closing the door behind him. I fell asleep, and when I woke up, I remembered what had happened. I told myself that it was all a foolish nightmare, but I could not maintain my self-deception for more than two minutes. It had actually happened. I thought it over and blamed myself for being a coward. If only I had screamed at him, "You base man! Do you mean to say that my father is a woman, and he disguises himself in men's clothing to protect himself from the fishermen, the brigands, and those who hate foreigners? Do you mean he lived with us here as a man, and he disappeared in order to show himself there as a woman? That he himself was that water nymph? That the tribe killed her after he violated their borders? Are you saying I'm a child from Umm al-Jurukh? And, according to your reckoning, that my father did not disappear, but rather he was stripped naked to be exposed to the people as the woman he really was? But there was someone who interrupted that plan by cutting off the head so the shame would not attach to the entire hospital?"

Because I was loyal to my vow to him not to spread the news, I just told Baghdadli, who caught him a little before noon as he was washing his mule under the rocket.

"Are you trying to tell a girl that her father was her mother? Do you find all that so funny?" Baghdadli called down from high above his head, just as a gust of wind surrounded her. She had climbed atop the rocket, which, over time, had come to look like a finger of stone growing from the earth. Her height and the elevation of the rocket made her words all the sharper and more piercing. I was standing behind her. I did not wait to hear the entire conversation. Descending, I stumbled and fell, landing square on my forehead. A handful of dirt went into my ears and nose. I don't know why I was in such a rush or which direction I had chosen when I tried to climb down from the rocket. All I remember was that I ended up on the ground, and I sat up with a crazy thought in my head, the last arrow in the quiver of my depravity. And I never sank to such depths after that—or so I believe.

My plan was as follows: I had heard that foreign men had been exiled by the order of the sultan upon two occasions. In both cases, a woman had gone up on the roof, above the heads of the Mohammedans, and claimed that she wanted to convert to their religion. She did not just say it in an easy manner, but she tore her clothes and bared her breast to the sky. She uttered Qur'anic verses and the holy names, and she called upon the praying faithful as they came out of the mosque at that moment, especially the men, saying, "This man is detaining me in his house. He brought me from across the seas, and now I've seen the light and received divine guidance here. I am your daughter, and I do not want to return to my country. Save me from injustice and distress! This man is tormenting me and plunging me in degradation." By *this man*, she meant her husband or her foreign employer. Then she went on: "How can you bear your new sister in God to go to sleep while oppressed in her rights, unable to pray or to cover her hair properly?" And when the foreign lady finished, the entire city was in an uproar to help her. They celebrated and praised God that she was entering their world, while her foreign husband was arrested or driven out.

I did not claim that Davenport abducted me and carried me back to what I had been after God had blessed me with guidance and conversion. But after returning to the hospital and climbing to the balcony outside my room, I did claim, crying aloud to the people, "Davenport has confined three converts—Charlotte, Baghdadli, and Madelena—in Strangers Hospital. He is tormenting us and pouring burning wax every night onto our fingernails so that we might abandon our new insight! But we are resisting and defying him. Help us, O brothers!"

I finished my appeal. I expected to find a crowd of men applauding me. And when that didn't happen, I repeated the call a few more times from our balcony. It took only four hours of waiting before people began gathering at the door of the Strange Caravansary, which was the former building on the spot upon which the hospital had been built, a resting place for travelers. When Davenport bought it and turned it into a cotton-and-wool gin, the people called it the Strangers Gin, referring to the girls who ran the cotton gin. Those girls weren't actually foreign to those parts, but the term *stranger* still clung to that location. But I was a foreigner and a stranger in that city, and for that reason, I interpreted the cries of the people in front of the hospital as being intimately connected to me. The crowd that gathered in front of the Strange Caravansary was calling out to me, "O saint of strangers!" Some of them were striking their faces as they called, "O Zaynab of the strangers!" *Fantastic,* I told myself. *They have even granted me a name.*

Down below, Davenport laughed as I went on cursing him and watched the group that was gathering together to save me. I believed my own words and was convinced that I had actually converted. I once heard that Mohammedans had a tail, or the remnants of a tail, and I actually stretched my hand to feel my butt to see whether a tail was growing yet or whether that would come later. But that wasn't the reason for Davenport's schadenfreude.

When the number of people had multiplied and they began surging about, their compass heading changed, and they thronged past the hospital. Within a few moments, they were gone, and I felt a twinge of shame jabbing into my entire existence. The people had not come to rescue their recently converted—or *allegedly* converted—Mohammedan daughter. It did not seem that my lie had deceived anyone or that any of them had even heard my cries.

"These people are celebrating their religious rites," Davenport called up to me. "They are recalling the exit of 'the stranger,' as they call the Prophet's granddaughter, and her travels from Iraq to Syria more than a thousand years ago, after people killed her brother and his infant son." Davenport wanted me to know I was not "the stranger" referred to in the hymns of these grief-stricken people. Likewise, my new name was not *Zaynab*. My name remained Charlotte, just as it had been. I was distressed to lose the name that had brought me such happiness, even though it hung from my neck for only an instant. It flew away, just like my own schadenfreude over Davenport, a feeling that transformed into one of deep regret. It appeared that no one cared much for what happened in that moment. Everyone was occupied with correcting a moment that had occurred more than a thousand years earlier. They were off to save strangers of the past. They cared nothing for strangers of the present like me.

Only a few minutes passed before the cavalry of the Qawnaq passed by. In their hands were whips they used to lash the air, producing a whistle even more vigorous than the whinnying of their horses. They drove among the scattered masses and plied their whips upon backs and shoulders. The entire space was draped with fear, and I fled to my room.

THE SAINT OF UNFINISHED TITLES

My father says that the only way to know our feelings toward a teaspoon is to turn our shoes around 180 degrees. I know he didn't mean that literally, but rather that we turn around and walk away. We say goodbye to the teaspoon, and in that moment, we will know how much we miss it. If my father's words held any riddle, and if by *teaspoon*, he meant the face of a person we love, then my father was saying that it was impossible to know our feelings toward someone or something in its presence. We can only imagine and guess at our feelings. It is hard to know how dear a face is to us when we stand in front of it, yet the true degree of affection appears after we say goodbye and we turn around. And our shoes turn around with us.

I wasn't able to make that turn and discover the size of my feelings because I didn't have both shoes to turn. But when I found my leg, I would do it.

I remembered that lesson when I was in my room at the hospital, studying portraits of my missing father that had been made by artists on the steamship during our journey to Basra. I realized I felt such a degree of longing that my fingers reached out to stroke the tip of his nose. I tried to lift off his hat and open his shirt to run my hand over his chest in order to confirm my father's manhood. Baghdadli and I got out the file for the water nymph and spread it over my bed. We reviewed all we had heard about her and everything the people had reported about her fatal wound, exemplified by slicing off her head and letting her float on the surface of the water without a face. The details in the record said that her weight was 180 pounds, which would be 190 pounds if we added the hypothetical head. Father Emmo—whose body had never been seen by anyone and who went to extremes in covering his body with clothes, coats, and leather belts wrapped in the hair of horse tails—was much more slender than that. Based on my crafty and immoral inspection of the water nymph's body, her buttocks, which looked like an overturned boat as she lay on her stomach, had no connection to the bodily design passed down by my father's ancestors, which did not cease to produce small, slender bodies that were cast into the world with lavender noses connected to their foreheads by means of arched bridges.

The thing my father did share with the water nymph was that white, almost blueish, hue, as well as a scent that recalled the smell of glue. To tell the truth, I never once noticed that smell myself, but the people made us hear about it, especially those who didn't know that we could understand Arabic. We heard them make sarcastic comments, though they never got angry. All our usual behaviors made them laugh, no doubt about it. For them, our arrival in Basra had been the entry of a monkey trainer with his little crippled monkey. We were the object of everyone's laughter, even the sick who were about to die from their pain. People never failed to add those comments about our gluey smell.

My confusion did not last long. During the hours that followed, I formed a firm opinion regarding Davenport's theory of Father Emmo being a nun disguised in men's clothing, as well as the nonsense about his being the water nymph. All that was finally dispelled when I studied a pair of women's shoes at the door to the administrative office and eavesdropped on the conversation inside.

One old shoe—its cloth stained by a map of salt, the decorative threads wearing through—and the other shoe of the pair, turned upside down.

The visitor whom Baghdadli had been meeting with for fifty minutes and who had left her shoe turned upside down had caught my eye. The quiet of the early afternoon prompted me to play a trick on the guards, without them being privy to my entertaining game with the shoes. They saw an evil omen in overturned shoes, and now, wanting the dirty sole to face up toward God, they were quick to return the visitor's shoe to its place. When they weren't looking and had hurried off to escort patients' relatives into and out of the building, I snuck up and turned the shoe back over. One of the guards noticed the shoe and returned it to its proper state, only for me to repeat my trick when they weren't looking.

As we were playing this game on one side of the door, I was able to catch a glimpse of the visitor's face, and I overheard her sobbing. Baghdadli spotted my head peeking around the corner, so she slammed the door and cut off my view. But the living voice had also been cut off, so I butted against the door and pushed it back open all the way. My eyes fell upon the visitor, who I saw was naked and gleaming like a silver pitcher. Previously, I had been exposed to Baghdadli's reproaches for studying the bodies of naked women in Strangers Hospital. I ignored her admonitions and went on studying this woman's proportions, measuring them and examining them with my eyes as I chewed my fingernails.

"Don't I look like one of the daughters of Umm al-Jurukh?" I heard her say, pointing to herself, stroking her chest quickly and slapping her cheeks. At first, I didn't understand the mystery behind her words.

Baghdadli was engrossed in the visitor's emotion and did not immediately move to obscure my view. But when the visitor resumed speaking, Baghdadli threw a blanket over her and threw another blanket over me to prevent me from seeing forbidden things. A couple of minutes later, she lifted the second blanket off me when it occurred to her that such an action was stupid, that as long as the girl herself was covered up, there was no need to conceal the sight of her from me. The girl spoke at length. She swore she was a village girl, one who had fled the grinding war that had flared up between the villages of Umm al-Jurukh and Dahrab.

"It's the same war that began when we were children. It cools off, disappears, dies, and then flares up when the fishing season returns and the waves rise. After a reconciliation, we marry them and they marry us. Then we carry off their daughters, and they carry off our daughters after the war." She stopped for a few minutes to check her tears and her coughing. The sense of surprise cooled within me. Even Baghdadli took a deep breath and relaxed. Here was the story, at last, and by the time it ended, the story of the water nymph had reached its conclusion.

"In the last round of fighting, the conflict lasted a long time. They killed our dogs. Then they killed our men. Then they killed our water buffalo. Our sheikh, Hadrallah, feared that none of us would be left after the resolve of our men slackened. Our bravest men had been killed, along with the children of those brave men. I, along with the rest of the daughters of the Hadrallah tribe and a small band of men, began to direct the village in his name. We tended its water buffalo, and we guarded its borders with our dogs at the fences. Some of the few remaining young men didn't like that. They roused themselves and nearly attacked us. My sister screamed at them and sang a long, sad love song that nailed them in place like mummies. They yielded to her. Even Sheikh Hadrallah yielded to her. Life began pulsing through our village once again. The village of Dahrab sensed that Umm al-Jurukh was still breathing. Once more, smoke rose from the cooking pots and the coffeepots. They attacked us and lay siege to our village. Sheikh Hadrallah decided to ignite the feelings of the men who remained with a certain stratagem that occurred to him. He asked my older sister and me to strip naked and approach the enemy. Naked as God made us, we would run towards them. Either the remaining men in our village would hurry behind to cover us or else the enemies would seize us, make us their prisoners, and violate our honor. This suicidal plan was one last attempt to keep our remaining men from being killed. In the beginning, I did not listen to it, and I did not believe that this trick of getting naked would revive their determination. But I could not stop myself when I saw my sister, the last person left in my family, taking off her hijab and then proceeding to strip off her clothing, piece by piece. The men and I ran towards her to cover her up. Her yearning to fight and her fiery zeal overwhelmed me. It urged me on. She kicked two young men and ran ahead of them to reach the edge of the village. She went out in front of the enemy fighters, facing them full-on, unconcerned that they could see her privates. She recited a poem boasting of us: of her parents, brothers, and husband, all slain by the daggers of the Dahrab. Then she allowed a moment of silence, which I didn't understand. She raised her hands and ran towards the enemy. Our men joined the attack behind her, wanting to cover her up or to kill the men of Dahrab. Hadrallah's plan had worked. I found myself stripping off my clothes like her and running behind the men, who pushed me up to the front. But someone pulled me by the hair and dragged me off to his boat. I thought it was one of the Dahrab men, but it soon became apparent that it was a youth who had proposed to me, and whose suit of marriage had been refused by my brothers. He helped me, threw some clothes over me, and hurried me away from the battle. He did not allow me to fight and to learn the fate of my sister. But some days later, I learned that the Dahrab tribe had killed my sister and cut off her head so that the waters would carry her off to the One-Eyed Tigris, and the One-Eyed Tigris would bring her to you. Hadrallah's plan succeeded, and my sister was killed."

"The water nymph," I said, as Baghdadli pulled the sheet back over my face to cover my gaping mouth.

That scene ended when a little girl came in. She ran past me impatiently, pushing me aside and finding her way to her mother's lap.

The woman raised her daughter to her shoulders and went out. The woman, the water nymph's sister, handed Baghdadli a large reed—dry, the color of walnut, as though the sun had cooked it in the oven for ages.

Without a word, and without responding to my cries and refusals, Madelena picked me up and brought me down to the pharmacy and locked me inside the medicine locker. She did it all as though she were carrying some inanimate object. For a minute, I felt as though I was neither heard nor seen. Using the large shelf hung from the ceiling, I spread out my large notebook, which I had titled *The Sayings of Charles the Otter*. I had chosen a boy's name so that I could write more comfortably. It was my intention to practice writing stories inspired by what I saw and heard here, and also to use it as a treasury of novelties, all those unique things, ideas, and peculiarities of the imagination that come to mind and might serve as the kernel of a story or an article. It was my custom not to write a title but to only choose one after I had composed half the piece, since I usually wrote without knowing the end goal or contents, and its image would become clear only after some minutes. I would write like someone riding a bicycle for the first time, who lets the wheels and their weight choose the path—or rather, to invent some path other than the one intended, which always leads to falling. That day in the medicine locker, a Saturday, I began writing something about my father. It only cost me five falls off the bicycle. I kept on with the text until its middle. Then I stopped to think about the title for that unfinished article. I began turning over possibilities like playing cards: "What If You Discovered That Your Father Is Not a Woman?"

Baghdadli locked me up in order to discipline me. She wanted to cure me from the habit of looking at women's bodies. She once declared to me that this was a big sin. Women should not look at naked women, nor men. Baghdadli may have even guessed that secret proclivity of mine for women, or my early, cold feelings toward men, which set me apart from the rest of the girls, particularly those I was competing with when writing for the magazine. Baghdadli punished me, but I did not ever repent of that pleasure. It grew stronger within me by smelling their hair and stroking the veins of their necks with a passing touch that no one noticed or suspected.

They locked me up, though I did not feel myself imprisoned until I started getting hungry, which was followed by a languor of spirits. Four hours had passed while I was writing, blocking out the chaos of the world around me with paper earplugs I'd made from scraps of patient cards, after

I tore away the part that bore the image of the King of Glory. When the earplugs fell out, the din of the market rushed into my head. My nose also happened to be running at the time. Was that what made me remember the door that connected the storeroom and the Confessional Room? I don't know. In any case, the Confessional Room was the symbolic name for my father's office, the name of which became the Siesta Office of the Assistant Deputy Vice Consul after my father's disappearance. My church did not believe in the sacrament of confession, and my father did not plan to retire there with new converts to hear their confessions. No one in this city ever converted, anyway. But the hours he spent in there with strangers and visitors did resemble confession sessions. My father would open their tongues with long periods of silence while they began babbling nonsense to him and unloading their memories and their daily chronic relapses into his hands. He would listen to them with a calm face whenever they paused to catch their breath before continuing the story. He would move his mouth as though about to utter a word, but he remained silent and just chewed his lips. That was the spiritual food they needed to continue without stopping. The tongues of strangers flowed like a ceaseless torrential stream, and things from the farthest forgotten childhoods, and even events that memory had blotted out, shone forth clearly in the hands of Father Emmo, or the "priest of the Mohammedans," as he was called by Baghdadli, who spoke freely with him, even though she was cautious of him in her own way. So the room officially became known as Emmanuel's Office and the Confessional Room among us who ran the hospital and its employees.

That storeroom did not have a table but instead, a metal board extending lengthwise through the room from one wall to the other. Under it was a square, wooden window for distributing medicine. For a long time, it had frightened me since its three notches came together and formed something that looked like the tip of a rabbit's nose. Small puddles would form on it from being washed with water that was stained with blood and oil. The iridescent oil glimmered when struck by shafts of the sun.

I expected Baghdadli would yield to the emotional telepathy I was practicing and that she would come—and in fact, she did.

She embraced me and pinched my ear. She reached her hand inside her shirt, something I had never seen her do before, and took out a piece of paper that she set down before me. It looked as though it was a receipt for transport and customs.

"No. Turn it over and read the back of the page," she said when she saw me study the titles and numbers on the receipt.

I turned it over and read: "News of the girls, writing exercises at the pen of the exhausted prisoner, called Khansar, who delights the eye and the intelligence alike."

According to Baghdadli, this page had been written with the reed that the water nymph's sister had given her. By doing so, she had established for us that she was part of the Overleaf Society, and her name was Khansar, which means *Pinky*. She had secret script she had been practicing since her youth, and she told Baghdadli that she had used it to record much of the news of the Shatt and its people, the Marsh Arabs.

"Why did she give you the reed?" I asked.

"So she could prove to us that she was a member of the Overleaf Society. And to confirm that she is not one of the pretenders. She asked for three hundred lira from me in exchange for all the exercises she has written, including the events, exploits, diaries, incidents, and archives of the wars of the Marsh Arabs, as well as their marriages, their animals, their poets, their celebrations, their circumcisions, and their tribal battles."

"Three hundred lira? That's nothing! I would have given her five hundred if she asked me."

"No. I asked her to recount for me some of the details, and I found that what she recorded wasn't clear. Most of it resembled old wives' tales and rambling gossip, slanderous things that could have been overheard inside a women's bathroom. I told her as much, and she became angry and left."

"We are losing the scribes of the Overleaf Society, Baghdadli," I said.

We began turning over Baghdadli's endless possibilities and suggestions as we thought about some way to lessen the weight of the guilt we felt for having neglected the search for my father. Meanwhile, I tried to pressure Baghdadli to summon Pinky again and ask her about the content of the pages. Suddenly, we heard Shathra's screams echo through all the corners of the hospital, as though it were the howl of some mythical animal emerging painfully from a volcano.

Shathra's wailing brought pain to the entire hospital. Her voice rattled all the windows, doors, and instruments like the buffeting of a noisy wind. I was terrified to look into her eyes, which would make me feel even more pain and cause me to lose my composure in my fear for her. Nevertheless, I crept to her side and saw her stretched out on the bed, with one of Davenport's hospital guards sitting on her chest. Meanwhile, all the rest of the guards surrounded her and held her limbs down against the bed. They clamped her jaw shut to calm her noisy tongue.

Shathra was sweating profusely and groaning feverishly. Her labored breathing stopped for a few moments. Then she started moaning and crying out again. There was no clear story of what she had suffered. Baghdadli had no interest in the stories of the strangers around us, nor in the tales of the guards or the locust vendor who had found her, lying unconscious on the riverbank. Waking her up had only brought her pain back to her, which she met with a scream that made that man's ears ring. He'd picked her up and carried her, along with his locust traps, into the courtyard of the hospital.

Baghdadli wrote in the register of injuries whatever people said. But the custom here was not to give any weight to the reason behind a wound or the instrument used to cause it. Those details were left to the police and judges if they came and asked. We hoped to avoid becoming involved in any type of interaction with the tribes of patients, nor did we want to be a party or witness to a struggle between a victim and the one who had struck the blow. All we sought was to heal the patient. And this time, the task of assigning the cause of the injuries did not lead to any responsibility anyway, given that the one committing the crime was an otter.

It was known that Shathra owned a small herd of tame otters, but what I didn't know until later on was that she used her otters to catch a great number of other otters. She sent them out like a kind of double agent, with pairs of doves in their mouths, and they would lead more otters back to her. Otter pelts were described as the very softest fur in the animal-skin trade, and it was the rarest found in the shops of Europe. Meanwhile, no animal had feces that smelled worse, and that product was used for reviving patients and reducing labor pains. No one knew exactly whom Shathra had sold her otter children to—or, to use a more precise expression, her otter spouses. It did not appear that she hid her activities out of fear of taxes or the shared profits and forced labor that Turkish soldiers extracted from everyone with a profession or a factory, from shoemakers, bookbinders, and coppersmiths to circumcisers, pumice-stone makers, and swindlers. Instead, she hid the secrets of her work from us for the sole reason that she was ashamed of it. When she entered the hospital, it was like she was coming home. At the door, she stripped off all the filth of a long day spent searching for the lost and hunting otters. She often imitated us. She would pull a sash off Baghdadli and wear it herself. She set my father's glasses onto her own face and adopted an air of sanctimonious seriousness. It sometimes happened that she snuck into our rooms and put on our clothes. Or rather, she did not put them on but inserted her body inside them.

Her face on the bed was so swollen and distended that her features could not be made out. Her head had become nearly as broad as her shoulders. I had never seen a wound like this, and we could not understand what had caused it. Other wounds could be seen through jagged holes in her clothes. We quickly decided that the locust seller's story was a lie. Indeed, we gently sent him on his way and helped him carry the locust baskets outside.

A wave of hot silence washed over us. Then I heard people screaming her name. The guards cried and struck their heads against the columns and walls. Madelena wailed like a Mohammedan woman who had heard the news of her son being killed in the sultan's wars.

Shathra was dead.

THE WHALE'S INNOCENCE

At night, the river remembers my name. It utters it with perfection after stripping away all the sounds except *sh*. When my age was two-plus-seven, people told me that this was the sound of water as it runs between the palm trunks and boat hulls. For the river, all names begin with *sh*. So when Shathra died—one night after she died, to be precise—the river began uttering her name as well.

The event of her going to sleep, as people called her passing, was considered the most perplexing instance of all those who ever went to sleep in that hospital. None provoked such a sense of marvel, since Shathra was known for her cleverness and her proficiency in training otters. For them to have turned against her and torn her flesh "is a sign that the Day of Resurrection is nigh," said one of Davenport's guards, the one sick with mumps, making his face swell up under his gray hair and causing his voice to come from deep inside a cave. "This Shathra raised otters, and they raised her. They ran behind her at dawn, hordes and hordes of them, as she swaggered out in front, imagining herself to be a captain leading his troops to the front," finished the guard.

Baghdadli did not mention my name, but from behind the door, she whispered, "She's gone. Shathra is gone." I didn't pay any attention to her because I already knew, and I did not want to hear that sentence ever again in my life. If I happen to meet another Shathra, I will not let her die. It had never occurred to me to imagine her dead. For a long time, I imagined her sitting in her usual way beside me, though this time in the company of my father. I longed to see how she would behave in his presence and what she would be like if the two of them came together. Would she show him respect, or would she turn him into a joke like she did with the patients? Because the death of a relative or friend made me feel a sense of boredom and disinterest, I was not encouraged to take part in the ceremonial rites, nor did I feel that anyone would miss me in making the preparations for the funeral and burial. I preferred to stay in the pharmacy so that the entire matter of Shathra could run its course. I spent the time writing and putting ladybugs on my letters, along with locusts, butterflies, and grasshoppers. Then, for all the letters with long legs, I added branches and leaves. My heart was hard.

Baghdadli set me down under the Abu Kishra rocket and left me there. "I really feel the need to search for a ladybug with eight black dots on its back," I told her. She did not hear me. She went to prepare Shathra's body so it would be ready for the mosque imam to deliver her to the washer of women.

After she was gone, I busied myself with writing an article I knew no one would make fun of, under the title "Do Rivers Know Where Fathers Go . . ." I left the last part blank because I had yet to find a way to round out the sentence. But the music of the title's words pleased me, even though I knew they had no meaning. I told myself I might find an appropriate word to put at the end, and I stayed up thinking of how to create a remarkable article, one that no one would ever suggest was written for me, nor that would make the people thank my father for having raised a promising writer. In the first place, I did not want those fat squirrels in the magazine's editorial office to call me *promising*! Because without a doubt, I wrote better than all of them, those idiots!

I did not like the title. Perhaps it was because all the moaning, crying, and outright sobbing around Shathra deafened my ears and scattered my thoughts. I proposed a few other possibilities: "What If You Discovered That Your Father Was a Silkworm?" Or: "What If You Discovered He Was a Marble Vase?" or "a Gypsy's Song?" or "a Tick in a Dog's Ear?"

I confess that that was all I could think about at the time. My own torrent of tears for Shathra was delayed for days. It's the same with me today. Those who are close need to make me feel that they have truly gone: a death announcement—indeed, even death itself—is never sufficient.

At dawn, Davenport knocked on my door. Before entering, he cleared his throat, just like Mohammedans do before they enter the bathroom. He managed to wipe away all the painful feelings caused by the past few hours, dispelling them with a single stroke. He leaned over my bed. Then he knelt down. "Your Highness ought to grant me the Medal of the Golden Shoe," he said, making fun of the medals handed out by the sultan. He drew a sheaf of papers from his belt. They unfolded like a curtain. He rubbed his eyes and seemed faded and exhausted. Then, like a skilled actor, he quickly recovered his feigned delight.

"I've found your leg!" he exclaimed, but even as he was breaking this news, I was looking at a face that inspired vomiting, burping, and blowing one's nose. All the same, I rejoiced and babbled, crying aloud. I was unable to control the current of violent emotion running through me. That caused Baghdadli to hurry in, along with Madelena, followed by the hospital guards. Everyone circled around him with curiosity and questions. He cut them off and put a stop to their words, making a dramatic gesture as though he were putting them all to sleep by magnetic force. He cleared space for himself to speak as he stared at his paper. He reviewed the page and studied what was there as he spoke.

"Where is it? Where's my leg?" I kept repeating, until I thought it was crammed among the words.

"One of my men found it with twenty other artificial legs. We have not yet determined which one is yours, but we noticed that every leg has something written on it, and you will no doubt be able to pick out your leg by the writing. Now I'll read to you the sentences on those legs, and I want you to tell me to stop if you hear something that sounds familiar. Here's the first: 'If you see me, I'm lost. Deliver me to anyone in the suburb of Redmont.' The second is in Spanish, and I used the wali's interpreter to help me read it: 'Carlos Emilio, 5679 JK.' The third was in Hindi, and my guard was able to translate: 'The poet says, If any of you think it right to write a letter to her, I'm your man. I lock my house and wander about every morning with my pen on my ear.' The fourth: 'Mast man of the ship Medusa from five in the morning until midnight.' The fifth: 'A prisoner with half a step; my journey = halves + waiting.'

"The sixth: 'This is the leg of Soldier Corbin—'"

Even before we could say anything, one of the guards cried out, "That's Charlotte's leg!" When the guard felt us staring at him, he lowered his head and took a step backward, as though deeply embarrassed. That sentence from Soldier Corbin was found precisely at the top of the leg, and he did not want to seem to be a peeper who sneaks looks at girls' bodies. And likewise, since this phrase was a secret, everyone in the hospital knew it, but we had mutually agreed that it would remain a secret.

We went out as though invited to a wedding. The assistant deputy vice consul went first, together with his guards upon their mules. But they dismounted, and we all jumped into a large riverboat. Then I jumped into Baghdadli's lap. Our direction was Rahlo's bower, floating on the Shatt. Davenport did not open his mouth with additional details until we stopped at the door of the watery brothel. He asked his guard who had been making inquiries about my leg to enter before us and drive out the mosquitoes and clear a path for the assistant deputy vice consul, free of dust and the smoke of the procurers. Davenport made his way behind him, patting his back and promising he would buy him three camel palms, which were the palm trees with fruit used as fodder for camels. Neither Rahlo nor her son were present. That palm-leaf house was empty of its customers, and even of its demons. It seemed to me a merciful place, contrary to my expectations. It was a normal house that said nothing about its absent inhabitants.

We entered a room without a door that was smaller than my dress pocket. It was dark, and nothing shone except for a faint glimmer of rubber: Madelena was embracing my leg and rubbing it with her veil. And here was Davenport, who said, “Come on! Let’s get out of here before we find ourselves in Zanzibar. I’ve heard that these houses move with the river.” None of us believed what was happening or that Rahlo had stolen my leg.

The guard related how he had come across it in Rahlo’s brothel. He was making his daily rounds, the sleep overcoming his eyes after the exhaustion and troubles of the previous day, which he’d spent pulling Davenport’s donkey after it decided to stop in the middle of the road. That did not usually happen with the noble Hassawi donkey that had come from the region northwest of Mecca. Whenever you walk on your own after a long ride on a donkey, you need time to recover your footing and walk like a person again. Exhausted and with his strength failing, he was dragging his body along, not actually hoping to come across anything, despite his usual luck in finding things, as he said. He was mulling over his intention to return to his master as he did every day and make the short report: “No trace of the priest, Father Emmo, sir, nor the leg of his daughter.” Then he would go to sleep with his family.

On the Shatt, he noticed a boy younger than four, with half his body immersed in the water, who was frozen in place and staring at him. The guard understood the boy was trying to get his attention. The boy appeared intent on moving into the heart of the One-Eyed Tigris while keeping his face fixed upon the guard. He walked backward without his body sinking farther under the water, even when he reached the middle of the river. He turned to look back once when he got into his boat and motioned for the guard to follow him. He rowed for some minutes until he reached Rahlo's place. He stood in front of it, and when the guard approached him, he circled around behind the bower and disappeared.

Meanwhile, the guard continued his story greedily, as though his mouth itself took delight in the words. I noticed Baghdadli stroking her cheeks. That was not usually something she did when she was distressed about something or sad about someone who was lost. On the contrary, she did that when she was on fire with positive emotions and was carried away with spiritual enthusiasm. In that state, she whispered to me, "Khando! It's Khando!" She believed the boy was Saint Khando, whom she was devoted to. Who else? In her view, people played around and won their desires only through him.

"God bless your holiness, O faithful beloved of Jesus! Our little martyr with great glory," intoned Baghdadli.

The guard continued the story of my leg.

He entered the house of iniquity and found a pool of blood that was smeared across the floor into the rest of the rooms. The injured person whose blood had bubbled out to draw those lines had wandered about, searching for their bed in order to fling themself upon it. The guard was baffled by this scene for only a few minutes before Janah appeared, holding a dagger. He screamed at the guard and told him to leave. Then he strode over to his mother, whose sightless eyes had been gouged out. Then she slunk through every corner of the house, searching for her bed, which her son, before undertaking his deed, had dragged into another room.

The news reached Davenport that the leg was with Janah and that Rahlo was groaning with pain. He considered her to be dead, and he prayed for God's mercy upon her. Then he rushed to Strangers Hospital after personally informing the wali, who hastened to send his soldiers to arrest Janah and Rahlo's fleeing daughters. They were bound together by the wrist and not separated until they reached the gate of the women's jail, where the men were thrown to the ground and taken to the Qawnaq prison. It took two hours for the dyers to arrive. They wrote the Turkish expression *olmaz* on Rahlo's door, meaning *proscribed*. Whoever found that word on their goods or their shop or house would have their life turned upside down. If they were not eaten by the prison lice, they would be struck with permanent sorrow from the anxiety of taxes and penalties. What I didn't understand was why that word, *olmaz*, had been written on the foreheads of a troop of otters that I once observed being brought out of a smuggler's ship. Indeed, I saw the same word written on the stomachs of some of Shathra's otters.

Janah's mother was brought to a French doctor who was famous throughout the harbor for his dexterity. He wrapped a thick bandage over her face, telling her, "This dressing will prevent you from seeing for a few days. You must be patient and endure!"

When Baghdadli heard that, she sighed out the anxiety she had been holding. She asked the guards to bring the blind prostitute to Strangers Hospital. "The drunken sailor doctors will kill her!" she added. She corrected Davenport and asked him to stop praying for God to have mercy upon her soul, since his guard did not say she had died. Fate had not decreed him to understand that she was already blind. There was no need for the doctor to fear she would lose her sight, just as there was no need for her son to pluck out her eyes.

Before the guard found the legs stacked in the basement room under the house, they had been under a shallow layer of dirt that was not more than a few feet thick. The walls of basements did not normally stand up for long before underground water filled them in and the roots of palm trees broke them down. But that cellar was stronger than rooms of stone because its columns were made of bone. Once the story spread of Janah plucking out his mother's eyes, the news came out that the son of the blind prostitute had made off with the dead whales that had accidentally wandered into this bay and were swept into the upper regions of the One-Eyed Tigris. He did not spend any effort in wrestling with the whales to kill them. He waited until they killed themselves, and then he stuffed their insides with stolen property, which he harvested on his own from its owners, or which he bought from thieves. He buried the whales near his mother's hut, interring them beneath it and opening a door from their mouth that led to the lower part of the house, and their cavity became like a cellar. It often happened that soldiers of the Qawnaq caught him by surprise as he was sleeping in the belly of a whale with the stolen property, but each time, he ascribed the stolen property in the whale's belly to the whale, saying that the creature had swallowed it all while swimming up the Shatt, plundering the people on shore or taking things from the surface of the river. In this way, Janah got out of the charge and was free of suspicion.

Apparently, the whale had swallowed my leg, not with its mouth but with the fingers of Janah. The rest of the story, as Baghdadli saw it, was that Saint Khando had exposed the secret of Janah and his gang, thereby closing the whale's belly and preventing it from swallowing any more of the people's things and their property. Before his affair became public, Janah demonstrated his wickedness by gouging out his mother's blind eyes. His mother had seen his mean streak before, like the time he'd slept with one of the girls and kicked her in the stomach. There was nothing for the girl to do but complain to Rahlo, who did what she did every time someone complained about her son: She walked over to him and took a deep whiff of his odor. Then she reached over and grabbed him by the neck. She dragged him to the water, jumped in with him, swam along the banks of the house until she reached the hill of the Abu Kishra rocket. There, she pulled out of her pocket a piece of soap bigger than his head, along with a handful of fibers. She rubbed his entire body, stuffing the luffa into his armpits and between his buttocks. She would sing while Janah would cry out from the foam of the olive oil soap stinging his eyes. Then his anger would subside while his mother disciplined him by scrubbing his body with the luffa until he turned red and a new skin appeared, purified of all Janah's vile deeds. Janah would be restored to his original state—the tractable boy, calm and obedient.

Davenport had the rest of the story. He came with us the next day to Janah's hastily convened trial at the hands of the Qawnaq's judge. Rahlo was there, bloody and clinging to the hip of one of her girls. The strangest thing present for the session, situated alongside Baghdadli and ourselves, was the whale, settled in its final sleep. People had dragged it there, together with all the troubles, the goods, the property, and coins that it contained. Salt and ammonia poured out of its cracks. Janah had coated its insides with several layers of the two materials so that he wouldn't constantly breathe the odor of its decay.

The judge asked Rahlo to stand up and recite her injustice and what it was she sought from the wali's mercy. She complied with his order and stepped forward, leaning upon her daughters. She asked the judge to release her son, declaring that she forgave him. "This hairy boy is my poor dear son, Janah," she said. "I gave birth to him with an extra bone in his head that kept driving him to recklessness and wicked deeds as he grew up. Then my milk entered his nostrils when he was a baby, and that made him crazy." It took her a very long time to get all that out because she kept blowing her nose and soaking her sleeves with her tears. It did not appear that anyone was persuaded by her account, for Janah, whom she was defending and forgiving, was not at all as she described. The separation between him and the normal youthful recklessness was a thousand and one miles. No one had ever heard that he was crazy or dim-witted. He'd won the people's affection and kept it until the very moment he was surrounded by the Qawnaq police and his fate was in their hands.

In everyone's eyes, Janah was a good boy, but he had acted from an old spite or because of a youthful recalcitrance that suddenly appeared. Rahlo wept when Baghdadli approached her and said she'd heard the beating of Janah's heart and that all she saw in her boy was a cowardly child who flitted here and there like a horsefly. In less than a quarter of an hour, all Rahlo's emotions were thrown into confusion. She spoke words that did not make any sense, and the judge ordered her to be taken from the square, where the trial was being held.

The wali tormented neither the people's minds nor their curiosity. His guards scraped the whale and split open its belly. First, they took out the majority of things connected to stolen property, like chairs, chess sets, helmets, and cages with their dead monkeys. And since the people were like me in not wanting anyone to spoil their fantasy, they were displeased when the wali's secretary said with a laugh, "There are no prophets and no priests in the belly of this whale. You can all go home to your beds!"

"And no Father Emmo?" I said to myself.

Attending the trial and ensconced in the front rows were the wali's elite, the tribal chiefs, the priests of the Carmelite Church, and students of sharia law, together with their sheikhs from the Fatuhi School. The general masses and barefoot populace remained at the back of that large circle of notables, without any cushions to sit on, for they felt that secretary's words did not concern them. We were not actually waiting for a prophet to come out to us from the belly of the whale. But we were afraid of the idea. None of the people listened to orders. They crowded together, surged forward, and created general chaos in that place, so the wali ordered them to be disciplined with whips until they were dispersed. At that point, the belly of the whale was still promising lost things. The police were rummaging through it, and strange curiosities were falling out, including some copies of the Gospel. Yes! After all this time, I was seeing the missing bundle of Gospels. My running-away Gospels. The path between them and me was clear, and I made a run for them, caring nothing for the stares of the people. I freed them from the lungs of the whale. Their wings were not spread, and no pages were open for me to read my fate and my direction. They were closed and wet with oil and grease. The words would have been in good condition were it not for the tears of running ink. A little girl struggled with me over the Gospels, which I found unaccountably strange, until my eye fell upon the prayer books and volumes of the Qur'an that were placed among the Gospels, and I knew that she wanted to pull out a Qur'an. Her mother called out to her, "Watch out! It bites!" The girl became cautious and took a step back. I thought the mother was making a joke about the dead whale biting her, so I turned to get a good look at the woman's face. It was Pinky, but she was not naked this time.

"Which of these books will bite?" I asked her, my face flushing with anger.

"Books don't bite," said Pinky, "but hearts do." The sentence came right out, without a pause to think, as though she had performed the scene before.

After the stolen things were emptied out and the people rushed forward to collect what belonged to them or didn't belong to them, the fish collapsed, and its mouth folded over, looking just like the hips on a pair of trousers when they crumple and then lie flat upon the floor. The people remained in a state of high alert, watching for my father to emerge from inside it. But the farting sound that came from inside the whale as it toppled embarrassed me deeply and left everyone there feeling abashed.

Janah departed from the judge's presence and was sent to juvenile detention, where the criminals made use of the events to excavate rivers, pollinate the palms, squeeze date candies, and load red bricks. The old men parted, as did the pimps with their concubines among the wave troughs, aboard steamships and under the hats of captains.

Before darkness fell, Rahlo had turned her floating bower into ash and smoke. She burned her house and her clothes in the heart of the river. The fire in the night was as revealing as a lover's song, or so she said. I don't deny that I helped her do that, together with Baghdadli. Setting that fire filled us with happiness, and its smoke isolated us from all others, as though there were no one in the whole world but us three.

THE FOURTH QUARTER

THE IDLERS' HILL

We were in the cart. Baghdadli pierced one of the pimples on my forehead with a fishing hook that she pulled out of her veil. I went out with her, celebrating my long-awaited leg with all the cooing of the doves inside my chest. It was understood that her fishhook would hurt, but the plodding of the mules numbed my face. A ladybug walked along her sleeve and paused on her wrist. I grabbed her other hand to stop her. I picked up the ladybug and drew it close to my face so that I could count the black spots on its shell. One, two, three, four, five, six, seven. "Seven, Baghdadli. There are seven." She gave me the fishing hook as she raised her eyebrow, and I knew what I had to do. I held the ladybug between my index finger and thumb and pierced its left side, giving it one more black spot. "Eight," we said together. Eight, yet Father Emmo did not appear, nor did he stand on his hands like he'd promised.

◆ ◆ ◆

"Sister, is this sweet thing, God preserve him, the son of Father Emmo?" asked the cart driver, who turned around after hearing me cry out.

"Yes," she replied. "His son is not all there in the head."

She slapped me on the leg, celebrating its recovery, but also as though she was reproaching me for putting her hip to use as my wheelchair for all those days. We passed by the livestock market to buy a sheep to sacrifice as an offering to young Saint Khando and to distribute its meat to the poor. Baghdadli believed that Saint Khando was the one who had returned my leg by enticing Davenport's guard to follow him all the way to Rahlo's house.

Now we were quarreling over the choice of the best sheep. I was insisting on the prettiest one, and she was insisting on the fattest one. That went on until the conflict was decided in my favor.

I buried a ladybug at the back of the sheep's skull when an idea occurred to me. I suggested to her that we go ourselves to Enervated Island and distribute two sheep there to the enervated and idlers who were despised by the people and writhed with hunger. These two groups were considered lower than the poor and a little less miserable than the lepers. The enervated were those stung by an insect known as the deer tick. Despite its beautiful name, the tick left its victims in a state of utter lethargy from the burning pain of infected blood. On top of all that, they suffered from great hope, an embrace of life, and a spirit capable of planning for the coming days, despite the absolute immobility that opposed them in all things. As for the idlers, they were of a certain kind of reputation, conscience, and smell. They were small in number and fully awake, but their motives for life and their usual duties had fallen away. The idler, in the moment that the Turks brought that word here, was torn out of their dictionaries and distributed among these markets. Most often, the idler was not able to stand up. He felt oppressed even from opening his eyes or cleaning himself after defecating. If he noticed someone, he would ask them to bring him water even if the cup was only half a meter away.

We proceeded with our two sheep. A police officer came up to us to collect the tax, which was six qirsh. Baghdadli gave him three and promised to give him the sheep's head in exchange for the rest, an offer accepted grudgingly. The five of us set off for the Hill of the Idlers and the Enervated. By *five*, I mean me, the two sheep, Baghdadli, and the police officer, and by *hill*, I mean a spot surrounded by water on three sides and connected to the shore by a line of banana trees extending over the motionless water. We were beaten there by the Mohammedan butcher who was going to slaughter the sheep according to the teachings of the people in that city, just as Baghdadli had requested. The butcher stood facing Mecca and recited the two professions of faith. The police officer received the head of the first sheep and then went on his way. Baghdadli rolled up her sleeves and beat the butcher to the tasks of cutting the meat, stripping off the wool, and breaking the knee joints of all four legs. The butcher remarked that she did not allow him to do his job after the slaughtering, such as cutting, stripping the hide, and directing the blood down the slope. So he began slaughtering the second sheep while Baghdadli was engrossed in the first. Whenever she severed a joint, she lifted it up and gave it to me. I thought I would leave that hill with what I might call a sheep dictionary. She raised her hand from its haunch and said, "This is the thigh banana," and then the "kidney house," and "the belly watermelon," and the "rib cucumber," and the "belly flank." When the butcher raised his knife from the second, one of the enervated turned to us and cried, "It's not permissible to eat this sheep, the second. Don't get close! It must be buried immediately."

The enervated said that with a distracted air and finished the second half of his sentence after turning and resuming his former position, staring off into space. The butcher became angry and said, "Why do you forbid eating this sheep? I did my job right. I invoked God's name and thanked God and turned it to face Mecca."

The enervated answered, "My son, listen to me! I'm a student of the Fatuhi School. Don't be deceived by my appearance and the pimples on my face. My beard was longer than this pointed nose of yours. When you cut the jugular in the sheep's neck, you have to make certain that it makes one last kick. Otherwise, it was dead before you slaughtered it. I did not see it move. It was entirely still as you slit its throat and cut off the head." The butcher quickly submitted to the view of the mendicant sheikh and threw the sheep into the river. The animal looked like it had committed suicide or died of a heart attack before reaching the knife blade. Baghdadli whispered an apology to Saint Khando. "Don't worry, Khando. I'll make it up to you next month." It was as though she was referring to the monthly salary she would receive from her brother Khando. We wandered around the idlers and enervated, distributing the meat among them. We would throw it into their laps or stamp their languid heads with it without seeing any curiosity or interest from them. The last part of the sheep was the tripe and the intestines. This went to a youth sitting on the corner of the hill reserved for young people. His feet were in the water, and his medium-sized chest was open to the sun. When we approached him, Baghdadli covered her face. I am not able to pick out handsome men. Rather, let's say I'm not skilled at doing so, but I read from Baghdadli's hesitation and confusion that this lovely idler was hard for women to look at without smiling involuntarily. His beauty prompted a flirtatious smile that could not be held back by the hijabs, veils, and robes of nuns. He finally did us the favor of turning toward us after we put the last gift of the sheep beside him. A sudden burst of activity ran through him when he saw Baghdadli, and he said in English, "Thank you, sisters." It was as though he was hinting to us that he was educated and that he could tell our identities from Baghdadli's clothes and that we belonged to Strangers Hospital.

"Benefactors! This is raw meat you are sharing out to us. Haven't you asked yourselves who will cook it for us?" said the beautiful idler. "And if you cook it, who will place it in our mouths? Well?"

Before we had finished digesting those words, he added, "It's not your problem. I'll sort my things out. But one last question, sisters."

We gestured for him to continue.

"I want you both to pray for me."

We murmured some prayers and invocations for him. Baghdadli began with prayers from her old church. She placed the cross on her necklace upon his head and stroked him repeatedly with it as she recited words in Syriac. Then she moved it as though sprinkling rose water upon his face.

He was suddenly startled and cried out, "No! I want a Mohammedan prayer! Pray for some substitute to take my place and for God to heal me."

Baghdadli kicked the idler in the side and pulled me away by the hand. We turned toward the isthmus leading to the hill. At that, the idler sprang to his feet and walked in front of us. His features changed and appeared more energetic, as though he had been struck by a bolt of lightning.

We passed a man lying in front of a woman, stretching out his arms and legs. The woman resembled the way he was lying on the grass under a shady mosquito net. Their absent eyes pointed up toward the sky. I was unsure how to classify them: idlers or mendicants. The handsome idler leaped up and volunteered to clarify: "An idler and his girlfriend. They are trying to fuck." He laughed. "Have been at it for two months!

"Father Emmo is my friend," he went on. "Before they drove me from the markets and the streets and the byways, I was the preeminent link between him and my leader. I won't hide it from you: I'm the leader's gate." He said that in a whisper, as though he were divulging a dangerous secret. Then he repeated the same expression in a loud voice to shatter the secrecy of the matter, boastful. Then he continued speaking, running along behind us. "I've tried to get treatment from you. I'm not interested in prayers. I'm prohibited from coming to you. I've tried many times to enter, but your sick guards knock me to the ground every time, and . . . I'm sorry to say it, but they spit on my ass."

Baghdadli said this was a sign that the idler was a pretender to the Overleaf Society, the group of young people who profess that affiliation and imitate the gang of scribes. There were many of these, and people got used to them, so they were no longer bothered by disturbances of the scribes of the Overleaf Society—for instance, when they pulled down their pants or lifted their robes, which was the utmost insult against someone's manhood. Nevertheless, people developed a way of enduring that shameful deed against them and pretending to ignore the fact that they were being mocked. "Even to enjoy it!" according to the handsome idler, his face nearly split open from laughter, revealing golden molars on both sides of his mouth. Those impostors kept burdening the people with bad handwriting exercises that did not approach the quality of the genuine skillful exercises signed by one of the five fingers: Khansar (*Pinky*), Bansar (*Ring Finger*), Wusta (*Middle Finger*), Ibham (*Thumb*), and Sababa (*Pointer*). They claimed to know people's histories, and they set about writing pages that appeared to come from the Overleaf Society. Those pages contained the history of the city and its families but with invented stories, which they used to shame people and extort them for money. Little by little, the people built up their courage not to submit to their pressure. They helped each other keep their heads and reject what the spurious writing exercises said. Despite that, there occurred some infighting and some painful incidents between families and tribes due to a scandal or some event caused by those exercises.

We shortened our steps so that the handsome idler could keep us company. He chattered away with us, and we opened our ears to him like a notebook. He prattled, and we recorded. Little by little, Baghdadli came to believe him. He was educated and had memorized the Qur'an. He was good at memorizing and composing difficult Arabic poetry. How strange that she inclined to him and believed him so quickly, while I had to fight with my soul to make it believe!

By contrast to some of the fingers of the Overleaf Society who studied in Istanbul at Ashirat Maktabi School, the idler had graduated from Al-Sanayi' School in Baghdad, a school built by the sultan for the sons of the wealthy and the scions of the tribal heads. The idler's father was one of the most prominent people in the city and came from the family of skilled eye doctors. He was eager to declare his genealogy and background with scattered sentences, several languages, and dramatic eyelids. Then he fleeced us all for the sake of winning an additional portion of respect when the opportunity presented itself, even though listening to him made beads of sweat course like waterfalls down Baghdadli's forehead because he was so obscene and did not care who heard him or saw him. He recounted how he was excited by what he knew about the fifth man, Pointer, who was not only the index finger but also the head of the gang and the "collector of scattered prayer beads," as he called him. Then he advised us to stand in front of him, for Pointer was the riddle solver, and for a long time, he observed Father Emmo sitting at Pointer's feet. Father Emmo would visit him and take a seat, just like any aspirant falling before him, or any student in his first heady encounter with philosophy, thinking, and reflection, about to burst into leaves of writing and its flirtatious letters. "He was like those women atop agitated horses that whinny to be penetrated."

"The filthiness of his tongue increases this idler's attractiveness," said Baghdadli, pretending to whisper to me. He smiled, puffing up his chest with pride.

"No doubt you're asking why I'm an idler. Fine. I'm not an idler. And all these half-naked people here—they're not idlers or enervated. People want to brand us with a mark that alarms the masses so they won't gather around. They don't like for anyone to meet with us or to hear us. They call us the wali's idlers because he gave the order for us to be brought together here and detained us without guards. The hill is open before us, but we are not strong enough to flee." Here, another bout of laughter came over him. "Not because we're lazy, but because they have erected high walls around us. Walls of empty nonsense and ponderous jokes. Everyone laughs at the wali's jokes and his fat buttocks. He gathers all the writers of the province and asks them to write funny stories and jests about us. In the centuries and days to come, perhaps people will read about us in books in a chapter entitled 'The Wali's Idlers and Enervated.' They'll be amused at our entertaining news, such as this stale joke: An idler was led out to be executed, and it was decided that he would end his life by being buried alive. They put him into the grave, but before they piled the dirt on top of him, they asked him for his final request, and he said, 'A cup of water.' They replied, 'There's water in that jug over there; just go and drink some on your own, and then come back here so we can pile the dirt on you.' The idler looked at the jug, and he was too weak to get up, so he called to them, 'Just go ahead and dump the dirt on me.' Laugh! Isn't this sultanesque joke worthy to be laughed at? With a joke like that, laughter does not become something that effaces your manhood or is a sign of uncouthness. Rather, it is a sign of good breeding and excellence because it is laughter at the sultan's enemies. And I forgot to tell you: all of us here are acting. We play the part of idlers and enervated and the sick who inspire misery, disgust, and degenerate odors. In the end, we lose ourselves in the Qawnaq's reports about us, and we begin imitating them and applying their tales about us. Most of those you've seen here and offered gifts of meat are not as you think they are."

"Come see us at dawn," Baghdadli called to him. "We'll open the door for you, and we can talk further. Come! Don't forget!" Then, almost as an afterthought, she called, "What's your name?"

The handsome idler raised his hand, squeezing together all his fingers except the middle one. "I'm Middle Finger," he said with a lewd gesture.

We got into our boat, but we did not row. We waited some moments, gazing into each other's face. *What are we waiting for?* I asked myself. Then she started crying. *Why don't we go back?* My dress was soaked in the blood of the sheep, which would not easily be wiped off. But she pressed her hands into her eyes and wiped away her tears. Then she asked me the same question: "What are we waiting for?"

I did not answer. For the answer was Shathra. Baghdadli might collapse, and then fishermen and fodder vendors might gather around us as though we were hearing of her death only in that moment. As though Baghdadli had not washed Shathra's body with her own hand and delivered it to the caretaker, and had not gone to the mosque to pray the prayer of the dead over her, alongside the praying faithful. We cried for her as though we had lost our life guide in that city. Her task had not only been to find lost women and men but to also remind us of what we had lost. For with many lost girls and boys whom she had participated in guiding and returning to their families, she was the one who first announced that they were lost. She went to the family, who did not yet know that their son or daughter was gone. She informed them of their being lost, and then they hired her to search them out. It can't be denied that most of Shathra's occupations, generally speaking, were to come across livestock and missing boats, but her reputation grew more from her description of being brilliant at finding lost people—or rather, informing people that they had lost something before they felt that loss for themselves.

There was another sadness overflowing onto Baghdadli's face. "The boat of Father Emmo that brought Shathra yesterday came from the paradise of rest. It informed Shathra of death and took her with it to the other world. Both of them belong to the same good lotus tree."

The dead Shathra accompanied us on the way home—the news about her, that is, not her presence. Her journey and her departure were the talk of the whole river: the One-Eyed Tigris related her sudden, unexpected fate, which no one had been prepared for. The chatter of the fishermen and porters added salt to her story. They said she failed to train those water dogs, which should properly be called water foxes, for dogs are loyal to their owner. A fisherman interrupted and said, "Loyalty! A dog isn't your lover such that you expect its loyalty."

"True," said Baghdadli. "We are the ones who invented loyalty." She noticed that I wasn't paying attention to her and whispered, "What are you writing?"

I let go of my pages so that they dropped from my lap and scattered across the sole of the boat, where they were stained with the blood of the sheep. She picked them up and read in a low voice: "My dear brother and colleague, Saint Khando: My father is not a teaspoon. He is not a lost earring, nor a bracelet that has fallen out of a bundle carried on a bride's head. He is not a jar of salt, nor even a wooden stamp. He is a priest who is good at speaking about the Holy King, and he does not believe in your existence. I didn't ask you to search for him. Leave him alone, and don't ruin these lonely hours. I don't want to return to the Idlers' Hill to buy you another sheep because you brought back my father. I heard from Baghdadli that you are an impetuous boy, a troublemaker who makes rude jokes. Is it maybe because you didn't go to school? Maybe. Listen: I honestly hope I'll believe in you like this muddled former nun Baghdadli. Do you know her? She knows you, and she knows perfectly well that she is no longer allowed to believe in you, not since she converted to our church. But what can we do with her? Her condition gets worse with the passage of days, and she goes back to pleading with saints like you. Listen, and don't be childish. Yes, you actually are a child. Just keep away from Strangers Hospital! Keep away from this world entirely, from people—all the people. You just create trouble for yourself. Those who lose their little things are idiots. Even if you bring them back to them, they just lose them again. My father, for example. Even if you brought him back to us, he would only get lost again."

I thought Baghdadli would slap me or at least get angry, but her face was lost in silence.

THE FINAL CALL TO ALL THE OTTER'S WIVES

A telegram arrived confirming that Mr. Davenport had been promoted from assistant deputy vice consul to deputy vice consul. He put on a splendid party, to which he invited the nobles and notables. At the party, he appeared with a halo of glory above his head, for he had finally broken one of the four glass boils that enveloped his name, and now just three remained. We, however, never once met the assistant, the vice, or the consul.

This, of course, was one-plus-six days without my father.

Memories of him began rushing over me, and the signs of feelings of loneliness appeared on my fingernails. I heard his ghost saying, "Take me, and leave her!" This was a phrase of his that remained in my mind from an old story that took place years ago. I was with him aboard the steamship *Santa Marina*. We were passing the Cape of Good Hope when a detachment of sea brigands pounced upon our boat. They rifled through the passengers' pockets and sea chests, and after plundering our money and possessions, they ordered us to take off our clothes and sleep naked on our stomachs. Everyone complied, even the old Catholic nuns coming from their evangelical mission in Tabriz. My father stretched out beside me and covered me with his wing. The leather whip of a short pirate with a decorated braid lashed his back, so he returned to his place, pressing his face against the deck. When they took all the women to the cabin of the captain, my father cried, "Take me, and leave her!" They pushed the women up, and no one listened to him. Apparently, they suffered a light stab with a skewer and returned in one piece, without their chastity being violated. The pirates let us go and allowed a conflict to fester between the old nun with blood dripping from her ears and the rest of the women. Meanwhile, the husbands lay down for a long, collective sleep as though they were sharing the same dream. I asked my father, "Why did you scream at the man with the colorful braid, 'Take me,' when they approached us? You had your head down, and you did not notice that they did not ask me to go with the other women to the cabin. He spat upon you and kicked you in the neck, and it was all for nothing. They thought I was a boy. Isn't that enough for you to understand that I do not appear to men like a woman, my dear Priest Emmanuel?"

Some weeks after that, on our first day in Basra, a saw took a bite out of my fingers. I had not yet learned to cry in Arabic. I thought I was going to die, and that's what I told my father as he staunched the blood before plunging his needle into my skin to stitch the wound. Then I lost consciousness. I slept deep and was led away in my dreams. I awoke to a vision, in which I heard him say, "You will not die yet. My hunch tells me that I will be the one to die first." I did not disappoint his hunch, and I regained consciousness. I recalled those moments as I asked the people about Shathra, but I wish he was among us so I could ask him about her.

Among the various things we heard was that the otters had not been satisfied to bite Shathra's limbs and trunk, but they had mounted her after she was dead, circling around her, plunging in and coming out, trying to penetrate her body with their pointy heads. These amphibious dog-foxes are famous among the water animals for being a savage lover, and if more people knew about it, they would hate otters and forbid anyone to touch them, just like they do with pigs.

Otters have their complexes about mating. They don't do that peaceably, and they don't offer courtship, affection, or flirtation before having sex with their mates. They resort to force every time. They are not interested in females that feel desire, but they constantly seek a plump female that fights back. They swarm upon her in great numbers, and if she dies after the rape, this is the pinnacle of their pleasure and desire. They drag her body under the water and continue copulating with it. It is the religion of otters that their delight grows if their mate parts from life. The male becomes erect and ejaculates in the moment the female's soul departs during sex, when he plunges his key into the female's lock.

But what happened to Shathra is a story that was more particular to her. After the wali issued a law forbidding the smuggling of otters, and even chasing and hunting them, the Qawnaq police and the Fourth Division of Palace Guards spread out through isolated corners of the lakes and among the Marsh Arab tribes—that rural part of the city, which for so long had swallowed armies with ease. The two rivers met and fed an enormous lake, decorated by reeds, where otters and dark Mohammedans and saints lived. The police and soldiers swept in and beat dozens of fishermen with their nets, their spears and guns, and their bags of poison. They trapped a crowd of otters in a closed-water channel called a gullet, and they did not notice that those otters were swimming, leaping, and rushing about like ghosts, accompanied by a woman named Shathra.

The woman freed her animals from the gullet. She swam with them on an exhausting journey of liberation under burning suns, which, by chance, had all emerged from the underground piggy bank. The journey to escape into the deepest reaches of the lakes took her seven hours. She fled from dry land to water and from water to dry land. She was the expert of the pathways, the guide for the steps of the lost. Her goal was to return to Umm al-Jurukh, her first village, with its scent of the father and his daughters. At the moment she was getting near, Umm al-Jurukh had plunged into a battle to the death with the village of Dahrab. When it reached everyone's ears that Shathra was advancing upon the village with her otters, no one undertook welcoming her. Everyone was busy fighting and protecting themselves from the anticipated attack by the men of Dahrab—or else making a run for it to save their own precious life. Shathra's youngest sister came out to her from the sheikh's harem in order to persuade her older sister to go out and meet Shathra, who had departed the village, along with her otters, ages before and left them both behind. A conflict broke out between the two sisters over what to do. Emotions boiled over, and the sisters began grappling with each other in a violent struggle that revealed to the people of the village the full extent of the soft bodies that the sheikh's sons enjoyed. Both sisters lost their clothes and rolled around naked together until exhaustion overcame them, and they lay together without moving.

That's why Shathra did not receive the welcome she deserved—because the battle of the daughters of the molar seller did not leave the people any opportunity for curiosity. It happened that the annual flood season had pulled the rugged village into deep water to the south, restoring it to its position from ten years before, for these villages moved with the current. That's why people called this one Umm al-Jurukh, since *jurukh* is the word for the wheels under carts. The village was moving along, and Shathra and her otters hurried along after it until that race came to an end and the panting ceased.

It was up to the old woman, Fayya, to appear and put an end to the sisters' battle and bridle the enthusiasm of the third sister with her otters. After Sheikh Hadrallah had been killed, Fayya was the one who ruled the village. She had also ruled it before his death, indeed, throughout the sheikh's entire life. She liked to hide behind her grandsons, contenting herself with whispering in their ears and pinching their shoulders. That was her simple and inscrutable language that everyone understood whenever the village needed conclusive guidance. Her age was twenty years more than a hundred. She lived in a basket of woven sugar cane, which was carried by two of her great-grandchildren, either on their shoulders or between them like a heavy suitcase. At that moment, she stuck her head out of the basket and decreed that the sisters be separated, their hair untangled from each other's, and dragged off to their rooms in the sheikh's harem. Contrary to her custom and everyone's experience, Fayya emerged from the basket with her whole body, which had bent double and perfected the resemblance between her and a silkworm. Her thin white socks gleamed in the beating rays of the sun. She ordered the men to resist the invasion of the otters because Shathra was coming for revenge, as Fayya put it, whose orders spurred them all to clean the space of any traces of the sisters' battle and to get ready for the invasion of the Dahrab village.

Shathra was prevented from entering, and the village moved deep into thickets of the marshes, impelled by the men of Umm al-Jurukh as they searched for the rest of their men and naked daughters, lost in the previous round of fighting. Shathra and her otters were confined for a week, without any food and inside a narrow space that did not suit the stubborn otters' desire to move. Before that, she had liked to mock the wali's soldiers and had written *olmaz* on her forehead, by which she meant to tell her otters, "It's not allowed," that is, it's not allowed to eat Shathra, Shathra is not halal, Shathra is wrong, Shathra is impure. Perhaps she thought that would prevent the otters from attacking her if their anger was provoked. But otters do not know how to read. She was there alone with them until the sun fell into the piggy bank, and after they were seized by boredom and hunger, her animals crept toward her with gradual steps, filled with the wickedness of foxes. When they got to her, they began playing with her and licking her. Shathra stroked their backs. The otters ventured to nibble her. The flesh of their leader tasted good, so they devoured her. It is likely that hunger was not the reason they rushed upon her and bit her tender, round body, but rather it was the boredom.

Middle Finger, for his part, confirmed all these details that we heard from the strangers at the hospital. We resumed our forward progress, and so did he. But would that he hadn't!

Baghdadli, for her part, after I informed her of the news I had acquired of Shathra's fate, cried to me, "These aren't the deeds of otters! I've lived here long enough to say they are the kindliest of the Lord's creatures. If they have eaten Shathra, this is something they learned to do from the fables of the sinful humans around them."

The morning after our visit to Idlers' Hill, Middle Finger visited us, slipping behind the line of veiled women at the hospital. He was not in favor with Davenport's guards. On his head was the kind of palm-leaf cap worn by postal delivery men, and he wrapped himself in the kind of robe worn by Orthodox monks, embroidered with crosses. It was clear from his behavior that he was wearing it to get in our good graces, even though we did not see it as any kind of flattery. Not because he was completely naked underneath and his testicles swung about like the bucket over a well when he sat on the second step of our wooden staircase, but because his presence did not make us feel comfortable, nor were we Orthodox. We watched Davenport's guards with one eye and studied the strange appearance of Middle Finger's clothes with the other. He got off the stairs and began walking a little between the beds for patients. He stroked their heads as though he were blessing them. He drew out a staff made of a hardened reed and began leaning on it, as though he were an old patriarch carrying his brass staff. It was curved like a snake, reminding us of the staff of Moses, which had turned into a serpent and healed every sick person who came before it.

The first words the handsome idler said as he crossed one leg over the other with frightened eyes that watched the passage to the door were, "Of course, you know that I am not only Middle Finger. I am also a prince. My grandfather is Sheikh Mughamis, who ruled the city one and a half generations ago. He maintained his independence from the Turkish sultans for years. He was the first Mohammedan man to abolish jizya tax and grant you Christians a certificate of protection." He was referring to Sheikh Mughamis, who removed the tribute exacted from the Dutch, the fathers of the Carmelite Church, and the rest of Jesus's followers in the city approximately one century before.

"I hope you at least will be useful, unlike your friends," Baghdadli told him as she pulled him by the hem of his robe and led him to the autopsy room. She asked him to say everything that might be beneficial for us, "everything you know and don't know about Father Emmo."

He spoke about Father Emmo as he knew him, but it was not possible for him to know about his absence. Father Emmo was an English priest who had built a hospital on the Shatt. Before that, he had penetrated the veins of the river in his boat, traversing marshes, lakes, and canals; wandering among weddings, funerals, and the gatherings of laborers and farmers. He sat among the fishermen, telling them stories and curiosities, and imparting the advice and admonitions he formed in answer to their questions. For example, the story of the boy and the watermelon was one he told when a fisherman asked him why God did not provide him with more than seven yellowfin barbels every night. Father Emmo told him about the boy whose father bought him a big watermelon and a small one. On the way home, the boy asked his father if he could carry the big one instead of the small one since it was too light for him. The father granted the boy's request, but the big watermelon fell out of the boy's hands and smashed on the ground.

Another time, there was a youth who asked Father Emmo when the release would come while he was weaving a carpet with his daughters with one hand and shaking a silver jug of yogurt with the other. Father Emmo stopped in front of him and looked closely into his face, prompting the boy to rephrase the form of his question as a complaint: "When are the noons? When does the light from Time's Companion dawn? Meaning the one who begot Mohammed, for whom some of the Mohammedans here wait until he will appear at the end of the world so they can pray behind him, and against whose leadership Jesus and Ibrahim and even Adam conspire."

Father Emmo replied that the release was always near at hand, without clarifying that he himself was not a Mohammedan.

As for how Middle Finger met Father Emmo, that was a story in its own right. He spent his sentence in the large prison of the Qawnaq, in a vault set aside for adolescents. It happened that a former wali—and there were six walis between that one and the current wali, Kadhim Pasha—published a writ of pardon for ten prisoners, though without writing their names. It was a gift he gave to Father Emmo. On the occasion of the priest's blessed arrival to the city and taking up his residence there, the wali let him choose the ten for himself. I was not with my father at that time, but I am sure that granting a mercy like this would have gladdened his soul. No doubt he saw it as the first of Jesus's steps with him in this city, to save, through him, the necks of ten of his beloved children.

Middle Finger told us, "I was in the prison, and I don't know how he chose me. I know that he walked among us, distributed among the various cells, searching for inmates upon whom he might apply the wali's pardon. Half the day went by as we all waited to see those whom freedom would fall upon. He chose five, and I was the fifth. He noticed me just one day before my execution was to be carried out. But he did not inform me immediately that I had been freed. He preferred to play with me and make my heart pound a little. He placed his hands around my head and recited a prayer. Then he said to me, 'Listen: I will remove the sentence of death from upon you if you discover the opening in your cell. I'll give you until the morning. I have made a small opening in the prison for you to get out. If you discover it and come out, then you are a free man, neither condemned nor indebted. With these two hands, I will stamp your forehead with the seal of the Qawnaq.' Then he left me to wrestle with the hours. It was hard to breathe from the intense anxiety and my racing thoughts. I scrutinized the corners of my cell, moving inch by inch. It was a marble room, carved under a quarry. I wiped away the ghostly faces that I, like all prisoners, discerned on the walls of the dungeon. Where was that exit they had left for me? Where was the soft edge of the stones? I scratched at the ceiling with my fingernail. I pressed half my body into the wall, trying to stick my head into the ground and listen to their voices. Morning arrived, and I had not discovered the exit. My scratching did not lead me to any hope. Father Emmo arrived with the dawn. He found me dismayed and in despair. He said to me, 'You were searching everywhere, and you overlooked the door, which I left unlocked for you yesterday!'" Despite that failure, Father Emmo had bestowed the same kindness and set him free.

Middle Finger, whose name was Abd Rabbo the Calligrapher, joined the Overleaf Society, but not yet as Middle Finger. He needed to repeat all his writing exercises and do away with all the bad habits he'd acquired during the period of his pretending, for he had begun by claiming to belong to the society. Then they chose him, and his facade was transformed into reality. He repeated all the stages with his teacher. That cost him seven years and significant hardship for his fingers, which were covered with bloody blisters from the great number of exercises. That labor made him worthy of becoming a student of Thumb, who waited until the position of Middle Finger became vacant and decided to elevate Abd Rabbo into it. He became, according to the testimonies of the other fingers, an imam of Arabic calligraphy, that exceedingly difficult art that a person might devote half their lifetime to. And that would not even mean they were good at it, only that they were acceptable, and experts would not catch them making blunders in the balance of the letters or the harmony of their length and breadth, or their weight, or their magic and their ability to intoxicate the examiner. These examiners, a select group of people, most of them old, had a tablet of writing set upon the low table in front of them. They would fix their eyes upon it, gazing submissively. Then, after a few minutes of silence, they spoke their mind and reported to the teacher supervising the student what they were feeling. Was it an intoxication of the imagination or a normal inebriation? When it was Middle Finger's turn, the examiner said, "Your tablet put me to sleep. I saw the letters surging like waves, and I heard them make a music that ran through my limbs. I fell asleep for a few seconds, and I woke up happy." A rumor—denied by Middle Finger himself—claimed the examiner was masturbating as he gazed upon Middle Finger's dazzling script.

After that, Middle Finger entered another season of exercises until the time that he was crowned with the turban of calligraphy. He joined the other four fingers in the house of Pointer. In those days, we had not known the address of that house, and I learned it from the testimony of Middle Finger. He said the exercises did not all take place there. Sometimes the society went to public places. They listened to what was happening, and the words they heard became a long, daily practice. Then they would select a handful of exercises to preserve on their ship. Some of them would be overwhelmed by the majesty of the beautiful calligraphy. They would go to extremes in arching their letters and making them vanquish each other. The process of reading these letters and picking apart their talismanic lines would become nearly impossible. Therefore, some people claimed that reading past events from the drafts of exercises was not an easy matter, since most of the exercises were written with extravagant letters that diverged far from the normal rules. They added long stems and transformed the ends of letters into flourishes and ornamentation. Their moments of mutual writing began with words formed according to the rules. Then their heads would become entranced by the forms of the letters, and the majesty of the beautiful script would sweep them away in a collective rapture, and the letters would be adorned to the point of becoming effaced and turning into each other.

Middle Finger resumed his facetious tone, saying, "Not all people are able to understand our words when we get so excited and take their beauty to extremes and intertwine them. Nevertheless, Sister Baghdadli, that does not prevent us from our pursuit sometimes. They accuse us of prattling on about the honor of their grandmothers and their father's aunts. They don't know that we haven't seen their grandmothers doing anything. We weren't born yet! No doubt the former members of the society were their contemporaries, but no one forgives us. I sometimes feel that everyone feels they've been wronged by us. Merely a passing allusion to small details about their elders and sheikhs might bring terror and certain death to the Overleaf Society, or at least send violent attacks our way, the kind that end in deep wounds or, in the best-case scenario, bruised bones."

As he was going out, Middle Finger did not stop pleading. He let go of his monastic robe and revealed his naked chest. "Many pages have been seized. They took them from the most secret and intimate hiding places. They stole them by force, with fire and whips. Our ship,

Umm al-Shamat, was plundered too. They pushed it up on dry land so it would remain fixed in the courtyard of the Qawnaq." Muttering and grumbling, he added, "I won't hide it from you that we are seeking someone interested in the history of our writing exercises, someone who needs that history to search for events in the past, both recent and distant. We aren't striving for God's face, nor are we seeking any blessing, the kind of blessing that you know. Not at all! We yearn for money, without which we will not get what we need to fill our bellies and our pages. Secondly, and more importantly, we will not get what brings us pleasure. Writing is our delight and our aspiration. We have acquired these black inks from China, and our pens are made of cheap reeds that we cut from the lakes. Then we tie on some hairs from the tails of horses who are no good for riding. Our great leaders strove to provide our salaries by means of communicating with prominent men. Not all prominent men, but that type who was interested in searching for reality. Ever since the first Pointer, and up until the one hundred and eighteenth. Today, however, we pass into one of our desperate times."

That night, Khando sang to us. We joined him in the garden, his sister and I, sitting on a wooden bench made by my father. Khando sang, but I couldn't put up with his voice, so I pretended to be asleep and cried out to them, "A voice like a snail's fart!" They didn't believe that I was talking in my sleep. Khando's sister slapped me on the thigh and carried me up to my room. But soon I came back, pretending I had woken up. I asked if I could sit with them; Khando asked me if I still talked in my sleep.

"I've never talked in my sleep," I said.

"And I testify that neither you nor your father do that. On the contrary, you are the Emmo family: you talk, and the people sleep," said Baghdadli, making fun of my father's exhortations to the people of the city.

120 LIONS, 257 DRAGONS, AND 300 BULLS

More than a thousand years ago, or a little more and still yet a little more, there lived a boy in Baghdad by the name of Ibn Muqla. He carried his mother's name in his own. She was the most beautiful of the warblers, and the most precious to her father, so he named her Muqla, after that enchanting blackness of the eye. The gifted boy grew up and practiced calligraphy with a powerful teacher until he progressed by degrees through the ranks and became a minister for the Abbasid Caliph. He established laws of writing and the formation of letters. One night, he dreamed that the hoopoe bird of the Prophet Sulayman was speaking to him. He mounted its back, and it flew up with him among the cypress branches and taught him how to derive the forms of letters from the circles in women's bodies and the dots, turquoise, and Bedouin movements of cows' eyes and the feathers of peacocks. Ibn Muqla wrote the words of the Qur'an hundreds of times. He wrote an incalculable number of letters for the caliph to emperors and princes through all corners of the state, stretching from Persia, Turan, Iraq, Sindh, Gorgan, Armenia, and Azerbaijan to Khwarazm, the Levant, the Mediterranean Sea, and the lands of the Maghrib. In the process, he left dozens of exercises and drafts that do not say anything apart from disjointed sentences, the rules and mechanics for letter shapes, and the laws of writing. But he conspired against the caliph, and his plan to help one of the princes launch a military coup was discovered. The caliph dismissed him, threw him in prison, and set fire to his palace. Then the coup succeeded, and his friend, the prince, obtained the caliph's throne. He restored the scribe, Ibn Muqla, to his positions and his treasures, and Ibn Muqla once again became a minister to the new caliph. The matter did not last long until Ibn Muqla hatched a plot for a new coup and persuaded the grandees of the provinces to join the plot. But the new caliph discovered the matter, so he burned the minister's palace yet again. Yet the scribe succeeded in fleeing Baghdad. He came back disguised as a woman. He went about among the walis and the politicians and persuaded them to depose the caliph, since he did not think it right to conceal the secrets he knew about him. So the revolt took place and the caliph was deposed. Once again, the scribe became a minister, and he himself was the one who tortured the former caliph: his fingers, so skilled at tracing ink with the heat of words, rejoiced to disfigure the caliph's face. He plunged a burning spit into the caliph's eyes and blinded him. Then he seized all his wealth.

After only two years came the third time he was dismissed. People drove him out of the palace and threw his writing exercises after him. Slips of decorated paper were seen running behind him, swept along by the force of the wind. He disappeared for a while, devoting himself to writing and designing its rules. He rested from politics and from playing the game of thrones with caliphs. It was enough to play with words upon their lines.

Then he grew to miss his favorite game and became a minister for the next caliph. He waited only a few months before he began spying on the caliph. He entered into communication with the Turks and became their agent in order to get rid of his master. This time, he was exposed to the slanders of the Turks themselves. They betrayed him, and the caliph cut off his right hand and threw him in prison. There, he was not able to write or practice writing with his right hand. So he repeated all his exercises and trained his left hand to write, letter by letter. Although the ardor of youth had faded, the training did not cost him too much time. He held daily competitions between his left hand and the writing that he remembered his amputated right hand doing. His mind did not rest until the left reached a level comparable to the right.

The scribe rejoiced and was delighted when he heard that another Turkish prince was marching against Baghdad with an enormous army. He began to dance and sing. The guards heard him and brought the news to the caliph, who cut out his tongue and threw him in an underground prison, where no one would hear his singing nor see the beauty of his writing. He himself did not perceive his own writing, on account of the pitch-black darkness. It is said that the caliph cut off his left hand, and unseen by anyone, he began writing letters using his mouth or his foot, either biting or kicking the letters.

He remained like that until he reached his midsixties. He forgot the letters and their rules. He spent his final months battling the tumors that had begun growing on his back. Then he died, and they buried him in a courtyard of the caliph's palace. Then, after a request from his family, they dug him up so he could be buried with his tribe. So he was buried in his ancestral lands. His wife heard about that and did not accept it. She exhumed his grave and took him to her own house. The scribes of the Overleaf Society—or the "nape of the page," as Khando called them—considered Ibn Muqla to be their belated imam. They followed his exercises and passed them on to each other. They became different societies that sometimes splintered and sometimes united. Some scribes appeared who did not believe in the normal exercises of Ibn Muqla. They taught their pupils that words should be taken from the mouths of the people and their ordinary conversations. They said the best way to practice was to write what took place around them.

Waiting for the Qawnaq sermon, Davenport went up to the roof. We watched him through the crack in the window as he stretched his legs on the carpet and scratched his ear with a key, making it ready for the voice of the preacher, Qasim the Rooster, the Zurkhaneh Lion, that tender flirt, who ought to be heard clearly without any confusion or interruption. Rumor had it that some adolescent rope sellers were arrested for imitating his voice as they swayed coquettishly, making fun of him as he approached them. He blended in with the voices of the crowd and the harbor, which hid his identity entirely, and people thought they heard a moan of pleasure from intercourse. We also heard that many of the people praying behind the Zurkhaneh Lion went out after the sermon with erect members.

We were distracted from the movements of the deputy vice consul and his strange behavior as he waited for the sermon. The voice of someone hawking newspapers rose, making the air vibrate. He beat his drum and slunk through the alleys with his slave as he shouted his wares.

The vendor noticed Davenport from the gleam of his blue shoes, which shone in the heat of the day. He decided to praise the topics of his newspaper in front of him and to incite his appetite to read. He invaded his ears with the headlines, "The Papers of the Overleaf Society in the Mouth of the Qawnaq," "His Honor the Rooster Contends with Christians over Which Is Better," "The Counsels and Admonitions of Imam Ali to Improve Script, by Laylu al-Aswad, Known as Ibham, the Thumb."

Then the voice of the Zurkhaneh Lion rose to our ears. He divided his sermon into two parts. He spent most of the first part reciting a poem in praise of Lady Fatuha Khanom, mother of the wali. People whispered everywhere that it was the same poem that he recited some months before on the occasion of the healing of Nurbano, the Italian mother of the former wali, when she rose, safe and sound, after the green fever. It had been said that Fatuha, the sultan's mother, was the reason that the Zurkhaneh Lion was appointed preacher for the province. She heard his talent for preaching during the pilgrimage. His voice reached her while he was among the procession of the female servants, and she thought he was one of them. She ordered a meeting to be arranged with that noble lady-in-waiting with the loud voice and the impressive judgment. When he appeared before her, she was surprised to discover that the preacher was a man, giving a sermon in the nearby wadi. In this way, the Rooster found his smooth road to giving weekly prayers and preaching in the pulpits of the Great Mosque, using his great repository of expressions, proverbs, stories, and verses, as well as a voice that provoked people's desires and aroused their ears. His brother—another Dik, though he did not practice Zurkhaneh—helped him acquire that position officially from the mouth of the sultan since he was the Grand Mufti of the sultanate, and the sultan charged him to issue a private fatwa allowing him to kill his siblings. The older Dik issued a public fatwa applied to all future sultans, in addition to the present time, advising that if the siblings of the sultan showed any inclination to obtain the crown and ascend to the throne, then it was permissible to kill them. In this way, the younger Dik acquired an unapproachable place in the hearts of the praying faithful.

Baghdadli kicked me because I was scratching the ground with my leg and preventing her from listening to the Rooster. Hearing his voice was a pleasure unlike any other, not only for Davenport but for the two former nuns as well, the frivolous American and the frivolous Arab, and I was skilled at annoying everyone, whether I liked them or not.

As for the second part of the sermon, it was generally about nature and the prohibition against attraction. He pronounced the word and then clapped his mouth shut. The people disputed together, and then he clarified for them the meaning of the word.

"Gravity means the power in the belly of the earth to draw everything towards it. It is not the eating of roast eggplant dip with cauliflower, as you say. Shut your mouths, and may God save you!" Then he turned to the magical qualities and uses of the magnet, which, the Rooster told the faithful, is a piece of paradise, designed to draw hearts together. God sent the magnet down to this earthly realm to exist as a rock, and it rolled down Satan's head as he was exiting paradise. And along with his other good advice, he did not leave out porpoise-liver oil, which is a strange, white, gelatinous liquid and a treatment for all problems in people's bones and tobacco-filled chests. Indeed, it is a salve proven for all illnesses, including heaven's aphasia, which is when a believer prays for ages and receives no answer.

At the end of the second part, he did not forget to mention my father, who was constantly present in his dreams. "Father Emmo refuses to part from me. I saw him performing the ablutions. He had rolled up his cuffs and was washing his feet under a golden fountain that came down from the center of the sky. I ran towards him and greeted him. He did not answer me. As usual, he was lost in his own thoughts. You might say he is stubborn, but truly he is good. Without meaning to, he ignored me to focus on something else. I ran behind him, and I saw him line up behind all the praying faithful. I approached him and stood like the people, praying with them. An enormous hand, seventy cubits long, pulled me away from them. It shielded me from Father Emmo and the praying faithful. I called to him to draw me to his side and drive away whoever was preventing me. He did not turn towards me; he was too busy prostrating himself with the praying faithful. I called again and again until the voice addressed me: 'Be quiet, sheikh. Be quiet, Rooster! From now on, neither within the limits of the land nor behind the gates of heaven is there a man named Father Emmo. From now on, he is Sheikh Emmo.' I heard that, and a fit of weeping came over me. I felt grieved by my condition, and I said, 'O Lord, you have accepted that albino Christian, and you have rejected me!' How lucky you are, O Englishman! How blessed your lot and your ending!"

The mosque was noisy with prayers, which crossed the space and were repeated in the corners of Strangers Hospital, waking up the patients and making the fans spin. That helped the Zurkhaneh Lion press deeper into his thoughts.

"Sheikh Emmo began circling through the dome of the sky. I saw him surrounded by a host of angels and the coffers of heaven. I gripped my heart and squeezed it hard to keep out the envy. You lucky one! How fortunate you are, Emmo! There I was, grumbling with rage. The wind carried my voice, and the angels heard me. They paused and returned in their flight. Emmo descended, along with the pious saints surrounding him. He descended towards me and lowered his wings. He reached his hand into his pocket and brought out a piece of paper. On it, I saw words of light. The page had nothing on its back, no ornamentation by the scribes. He placed it before my eyes and then soared away towards the throne with his heavenly companions. The words were flashing and dancing before me. As soon as I finished reading them, they evaporated and changed into a lily, which I preserve forever in my mind as it speaks these words, O sirs, and declares, 'Tomorrow is the Day of Resurrection!' But it was only a vision seen in a dream. No one but God knows the world beyond and the events of the future. I do not claim to believe Father Emmo, and I don't like to frighten you with God's actual plan. God and his holy prophet have granted us a prophecy regarding the Day of Judgment and the Final Gathering, but caution is necessary. The wise believer is the one who learns the signs and does not ignore the call of existence. Is this heavenly intimation not enough to inform us of our current state and our final outcome? I repeat, and I say again, that I am not telling you that tomorrow is the Day of Resurrection. What I experienced was only a vision in a dream. It is not any sound proof! Not any indication of the Day of Resurrection!"

The Rooster tried to control the clamor of the people and their chatter, which kept rising during his sermon. But there was nothing he could do.

"Every day is a day for resurrection. The believer does not wait for the end of the world. Instead, he must be constantly ready to meet God in every moment of his life. The Day of Resurrection ought to be a day of delight and readiness, of familiarity and joy at meeting the Almighty, the Omnipotent. There's no need for fear! No justification for terror!"

But the people did not pay attention to the various expressions he added to lessen their anxiety. They left the mosque with tense faces that showed the marks of haste and the agitation of those short on time. It seemed to most of them that they were about to face the Day of Resurrection, which my father had announced in the dream of Sheikh Rooster, and that only a few short hours separated them from the end of the world. The Rooster's words had spun out of control. The people did not hear him deny that the Day of Resurrection would arrive tomorrow, nor his assurances that the end of the world was a matter entrusted to God alone. They hurried out to their homes and their shops. It was a slow beginning to a great chaos that would overshadow everything, even the color of the water, the smell of the air, and the hearts of the people.

The coachman arrived, together with a bundle of mail. The letter that should have reached me from the magazine as a telegraph arrived in a letter. It read:

> Mr. Charl-Otter: We have received your article under the title "What If You Learned That Your Father Was Not a Woman," and since we highly esteem your promising talent despite your young years, we express our regret that we cannot publish your article. Father Constantine advises you to write a three-act play. He will kindly undertake to adapt it, revise it, and cleanse it of your naive expressions. He will reserve a theater for it, and he will invite you to train the actors from

> the youth church so that the people of Washington here will see your story, living and breathing, and we will learn from your thrilling experiences in Arabia. In closing, he commends your bravery, my dear Charlotte, and sends warm greetings to you and to your zealous father, Father Emmanuel. We, the editorial board of the magazine, are very proud of your witty spirit, and we see no reason for you to use a boy's name.
>
> Correction: We apologize for the confusion arising from our last telegram. There was a mistake between the names of you and your noble father and Father Josiah, who happened to travel with his daughter on that date, which we mistakenly published in the magazine. We beg your pardon and forgiveness, and we confirm for you that Father Emmanuel did not travel! And as you know, he is with you now in Basra. Perhaps he is sitting this very moment on his stone, reading this letter of ours. Take care, take great care, in the care of our loving Lord Jesus, from whom all blessings flow.

The first letter ended. As for the second letter, it was a terse reply in a sentence of four words: "Not suitable for publication." I was appalled, for the second article was better than the first. It was something I had not expected, and its title was "120 Lions, 257 Dragons, and 300 Bulls." It was a true story about an incident I witnessed three years earlier on the surface of the One-Eyed Tigris. I wrote that the people on the banks of the Shatt witnessed strange animals sticking their scales and their trunks and their fangs out from under the water, but that was not something to frighten me. It did frighten the two nuns, who prevented me from going out. I heard the people shouting, "God is great! Have mercy on us, O Mighty One!" And I started singing, "O Ruler of all! O Lord of Hosts!", supplicating the names of the Lord.

"A blue dragon," I heard one of them say as he pointed at the Shatt. His companion stood in front of him, sinking to his throat in the water. He emphasized his words: "And that right there, right over there, is a white lion. No! It's a bull." I saw a small ship leaning with its passengers and workers, about to capsize with its heavy load. I saw blue squares dropping from the vessel, leaving behind dust. I asked my father about those terrifying animals that people talk about on the Shatt and whose ghosts I saw. He said they were tiles from Ishtar's Gate: Ishtar, the goddess of love and beauty in bygone times, according to the beliefs of ancient peoples. On each tile was the image of a dragon, a lion, or a bull. My father encouraged me to write the article, and I wanted to be as precise as possible. I began counting the tiles, the dragons, the bulls, and the lions from my window: 120 lions, 257 dragons, and 300 bulls. My lips did not stop counting until those tiles toppled the ship, and it sank into the heart of the One-Eyed Tigris. I listed everything I saw and recorded the details in my article. I even recorded the names of the workers, the tribal sheikhs, and their guards who watched over the small ships loaded with assemblages of the gates for the goddess Ishtar. Even the names of the German, English, and Turkish employees who circled in boats under fluttering red flags embroidered with crescent moons and crowns.

THE RIVER KNOWS MY NAME

I am not at all annoyed that my plot was discovered by the magazine, nor confused by the news of the correction that refuted the claim saying that Father Emmo had departed the city for Washington. I did not turn my head when I read the line in which appeared the hateful word *promising*, because the wind around me had turned yellow. That was not on account of my embarrassment at their letter. I opened the windows, and then I could only just make my way to Baghdadli's room. A heavy air swirled through the hospital, nearly preventing me from seeing. I tugged on Baghdadli's sleeve after I woke her from her nap and pulled her along behind me. "Wait for me," she said. "I'll carry you." But she changed her mind after remembering that I had recovered my leg. My one thought in that blindness was how I would see my father's face if he returned and how he would find me. From my gluey smell? But he was used to it, so he wouldn't notice it. From my voice?

We stumbled along through the rooms. It seemed that the air had listened, just like the people, to the Rooster's sermon: it had gone pale and was getting ready for the Final Judgment. Baghdadli's fingers bumped into Khando's oud. She let out a long, frightening moan. Neither she nor I had touched that instrument or even gotten close to it. He always placed it on his thighs and embraced it, pressing his throat into the oud's side almost as though he were speaking to it. He never let it out of his grasp, as though it were his impregnable secret.

We took the oud and went up to the roof, where the dense yellowness of the air let up a little, and we saw the disk of the sun appear faintly through the dark clouds. It appeared that Baghdadli found something inside Khando's oud that did not please her, or so I thought. But I pretended like I hadn't seen anything. It upset me to come between Baghdadli and her brother. I did not feel comfortable when I heard them cursing each other. I did not like to hear Baghdadli screaming at him after the curses had fermented in her head or embarrassing him by recalling his adolescence and boyhood. This time, she found no one who would not pardon her anger. In the cavity of the oud, she discovered drawings of fat women that appeared to be images from Khando's imagination. Drawings of the women's bathroom. At that, she started screaming, and her curses flew through the air. The whole story came out: Khando was not a musician, a fact which grieved no one. He had never composed a song in his life, not for Jesus and not for Mohammed's grandchildren. He tried several times to learn from teachers but had no luck. What could he do when his reputation for carrying the oud had overpowered all his attempts to make the people understand that he was still only learning. So he decided not to betray people's perceptions of him, and he went on carrying the oud in all his comings and goings. He submitted to the people's aspirations for him and began to invent stories about his false occupation. Because an idle oud does not create songs on its own, and because it brings in no money and does nothing to satiate the hunger of its owner, Khando resumed his old talent for drawing. For two months, he had accompanied a German artist who wandered the deserts in search of Sumerian monuments, the graves of the prophets of the Torah, and statues erected by ancient peoples who lived between the two rivers. He persisted in drawing everything he saw and also things he didn't, and he granted Khando the freedom to watch and practice. But he did not require him to draw the rocks, columns, and gates. Instead, he made Khando more interested in drawing imaginary monsters with beautiful faces. After the artist returned home, Khando came back, carrying his oud with its belly pregnant with dozens of sketches, upon which he traced taboo details, dozens of monsters, dozens of women of all kinds—princesses, noble ladies and sheikhs, Bedouins, nymphs—all ensconced inside his mute instrument. Frightening monsters alongside faces that were sometimes mild and sometimes alluring. He came to realize that he was carrying the key to his livelihood in that licentious hand of his. He was seized by enthusiasm and redid all his drawings on cleaner, stronger paper. He opened up to his friends and wandered about with them among the fishermen, idlers, and secret bawdy houses. His income went up, doubling and redoubling in a matter of weeks. He was delighted by that craft and discharged it faithfully. He sold his visions of terrifying monsters to those who needed them to be alarmed and frightened, and his visions of girls' bodies to whoever asked.

Baghdadli cried bitterly. It bothered me to have that sound filling my ears. I asked her to be quiet for a moment. Not because I didn't care about her concerns, but because her broken voice increased the hospital's darkness and the yellowness of the air. It made me want to cry too. But I also wanted a moment on my own to enjoy the imaginings of Khando, who ran away, his face breaking with shame, after he heard his sister weeping.

He had been about to come to seek protection from the yellow of the sky under his sister's wing, but she received him with tears of rage, which is what he feared the most. He went out, letting the putrid winds moan in the belly of his oud. Khando's sister had released the beautiful women confined within the oud into that fearful evening, and the oud was now free to cry.

Baghdadli's family was in the North Tigris—the True Tigris—not the One-Eyed Tigris. They were responsible for the production of patriarchs in their church. A boy would grow up in chastity, placing a monastic girdle around his waist. When he became a young man, he would become patriarch of the church. When he died, his nephew would inherit his seat. She herself had witnessed three patriarchs from the family move through that elevated seat. She herself became prioress of a convent until she met Father Emmo, with whom she took refuge. In his sermons, she found something that justified running away from home and getting a break from a house that incubated patriarchs who looked like the Mohammedans. Then she left the convent entirely and traveled with him to the south. She decided to place herself under the wing of our beloved Jesus, the Good Shepherd, whom she called "the American Jesus" mockingly, distinguishing him from her dark-skinned Jesus, who carried a sheep and had lines of virgins and priests following behind him.

Khando's crime pained her. It ate away at her interest in theology and her thoughts about Father Emmo, the lost American. Madelena and I spoke openly with her. We told her this was an exaggeration, a false sura of anger. I remember that we cooked her fish soup, and we brought it to her. I slept in her room, under her wing.

"A yellow sky, and a yellow soup!" she cried, startling me.

We slept together until a large stone woke us up when it broke the delicate wooden window and came to rest on the bed. It was followed by a cry that was unintelligible except for the words "Father Emmo." We looked out the window, peering into the darkness. It was Khando—the brother, not the saint. He had drunk half the liquor of Basra and stood under his sister's window, cursing and reproaching her.

"Who was it that set poison for the puppies behind the Church of Saint Ephrem?" screamed Khando. "It was you, Baghdo! Who was it that used to steal Father Emmo's buttons and sew them on my shirt? It was you, Baghdo! Who used to steal the patriarch's socks for me? Who taught me to draw? That's right, to draw! What local girl is possessed by devils? Who is it that had fruits proceed from her jawbone on the day the patriarch read to her the hymn of Satwamin Qalus Qurillisn?"

At this point, while her brother continued screaming, Baghdo—so that was her real name!—relaxed and prayed for him in Assyrian, which neither Madelena nor I understood. He kept stomping and kicking the ground, and his voice kept rising in pitch. He screamed as though he were screaming for the last time in his life. On top of all that, he did not forget to light his hookah. He sat on his oud for several minutes to catch his breath. He watched the dismay of the passersby among the signs of the resurrection.

People gathered around. It was a squadron of the pashas' boats. Their servants were passing on foot, with their mothers cheering behind them. In front of them was a red ship that would take them to Thessalonica, where they would spend their first year in the military school. We heard one of the mothers as she conducted her son and poured out water behind him to obtain his safe return, according to the custom of mothers here. She told him, "Come back safe, triumphant, and wise. I entrust you to God. May the Almighty preserve you in his eye, which does not overlook the dignity of the Prophet and his companions. Swear to me that you will not return before one year. I do not want you to see the Day of Resurrection here. Remain in Thessalonica with the beauties there. O Lord! Do not return my son to me soon. I deliver him as a charge to You, so keep him in store for me there. Do not bring him back to me before one year has passed. The Day of Resurrection for us is tomorrow. Let us finish with it, and then return him to me, O Preserver, O Conqueror, O Eternal One!"

Khando turned to her and remembered that he had come to reproach his sister and strike a deadly blow to her dignity, not to listen to the prayers of mothers frightened about the Day of Resurrection. He took a deep breath. His lungs gulped down air and smoke. He took his place beside the dark corner of Strangers Hospital and struck her by shouting the title, "Prioress of the Pregnant Sisters!"

His words about his sister's past fell throughout the hospital's wall with the toppling crash of a flourishing tree. The Pregnant Sisters! Everything that followed that was Khando crying, shaking his shoulders, and following the people as they ran and gathered their things and their families in preparation for the Day of the Great Assembly, when the heavenly trumpet would blow and the prophets and imams would appear to greet humanity after the drama of this life had concluded. His sobbing voice changed from a soft cawing to a painful rattle in the ears that lodged in his chest and was stuck there.

As for Baghdadli and me, we went back to sleep. I woke to her snoring away happily in the morning, as though she had heard the happiest news of her life and not that Khando had just divulged her very worst secrets, telling the frightened and distracted people around him that pious Baghdadli had been pregnant.

The sun was going about its business. It dried the liquids and the feces that Khando had left behind under the window. His angry words evaporated with the call for the dawn prayer and after the second nap for the drunkards along the Shatt. The city had beaten us in rising. The smoke of cooking pots rose with the smell of vegetable and meat stews that people were preparing for the Day of Resurrection. We observed Qasim the Rooster, the Zurkhaneh Lion, wandering on his own among the tents that had been erected and the gatherings of people who were preparing for "the Day of the Great Assembly and the End of the World," as he said. He had apparently submitted to the opinion of the people and their interpretation of his dream meeting with Sheikh Emmo. His words, which had run away unbridled, were stronger than he and they alike. He despaired at persuading them that the speech of Sheikh Emmo in his sleep was not authoritative, and that no one knew the news of the Day of Resurrection except God, sole and solitary. In the end, he believed his own lies and became more convinced than the people that the Day of Resurrection had arrived.

He appeared feebler and less dignified after taking off his turban. He walked, holding his rosary and caressing it as thoughtfully as though he were stepping upon its beads. The yellowness of the air was increasing, frightening the people and confirming the claim. What increased our depression and made the air feel even more unwholesome as it pressed into our chests was the sound of bubbling water as it rose from the depths of the One-Eyed Tigris, sounding like a cannon, as did the wave of collective madness among the people, who had lost their own names and were not called by the names they had been given. Some of the fisherman, who had not yet forgotten their names, commented that forgetting names was a sign of the Day of Resurrection. Some people among us grabbed their heads with both hands to keep their names from leaping out of their minds.

The yellow fog began thickening in the streets as though it had appeared and would remain forever. It was Khando's voice that interrupted me. He was drunk again. "Baghdo! Do you hear me, Baghdo? Yes, you do. Davenport is a sheep merchant. Your lover, and the reason we fled here. He struck me on the eye, and I didn't do anything to him! I only rebuked him for the wool that he stole, that blue sheep. Davenport doesn't earn money from sheep. He is here to buy a blue sheep. There are only a few hours until the Day of Resurrection, and here I am telling you—that thief of a lover of yours made you pregnant and brought you here so he could buy a blue sheep. Wipe the dust off the mirror and look at your pale face, so loathsome to see. Why did you think he would marry you? What can men see in your worn-out ankles? Eh? What I told you has happened. He made you bury your fetus, still wet from the womb. He brought you here and forgot you, and now he is running away with the blue sheep."

That was also what the guards said. They observed Davenport getting into a boat on his own with a blue sheep. But that scene lost its importance after a few minutes and seemed normal when the confusion of the people eclipsed it. Davenport's blue sheep was a famous turquoise animal of gold and jewels, known as "the Sheep of the Swamp." My father once mentioned to me that the Germans discovered it in an ancient Sumerian palace. It dates back thousands of years. The ancient sculptor designed it to embody the sheep with which Ibrahim redeemed his son, Isma'il, from the slaughter. In the coming hours, I would hear that Davenport had summoned his guards and ordered them to leave the hospital and go with him to protect him and the Sumerian sheep that he carefully embraced, taking advantage of the chaos in the city to smuggle out treasures to sell to prominent museums. The bubbles were popping around them. The dragons were sinking. In my sleepiness, I was overcome by yawns. I wanted to sleep before the end of the world. To get a rest from thinking about Baghdadli's scandals and shame.

I've changed my mind about you, Khando. Saint Khando, bring back Baghdadli, who is lost in her own mind. Let's leave aside my father for tonight!

The prows of boats were banging into each other. The river was choked with empty boats and ships whose crews had fled. A dreadful crowding took place, much like the crowding of my pawns as they exit the chessboard en masse when my father routs me in a game. All the flags were toppled and gone. The yellow extended to people's lips, which were dry from fear. Everyone was freed from the supervision of the police and the soldiers, who slunk off to who knows where. The city was devoid of any security men at all. But no orgy of stealing occurred. No one took any interest in the open shops, left without any guards or vendors, nor in the goods piled up along the shore. Even the sight of Davenport with his blue Sumerian sheep no longer held the people's gaze.

"Here we are, Sheikh Emmo!" cried the people.

The sun was setting, and the people waited for the call to prayer from the Great Mosque. Rumors spread about the Zurkhaneh Lion's flight from the present torment. But he put the lie to their propaganda by appearing with his parrot on the wall of the minaret. It was well known that he would sometimes conduct the call to prayer in the company of a parrot. The people circled around the minaret, perhaps in an attempt to recover their ordinary days, which were neither terrifying nor yellow. They longed for an ordinary sunny day, with the call to prayer suddenly reaching their ears. Some time passed, but they did not hear the voice of the Zurkhaneh Lion calling them to prayer. Half an hour went by, and he neither made the call to prayer nor came down. Then the hour for prayer was past. Everyone rushed to break down the door of the minaret and ascend the tower that the Zurkhaneh Lion used to take his bird in order to teach it the call to prayer. It was clear that he was not with his own parrot. Some nobles had started renting calls to prayer with the Zurkhaneh Lion. They would give him their birds, and he went up with one of them each time for the call to prayer with his exciting voice, which pierced the ears and woke the dead before it woke the living. The parrot, which he only needed to be on his shoulder, listened, and it would memorize the call to prayer in order to be able to utter it. The whole thing took only three days, and then he would return the parrot to its owner—a parrot that performed the call to prayer and recited prayers. On that day, the Rooster-Lion and his parrots were prevented from giving the call to prayer, and people boasted about the minaret.

With my own eyes, I saw what no one would ever believe, no matter how many oaths I swore or curses I uttered. A parrot flew and landed on one of those bodies covered in rice sacks and tent canvas. Perhaps it entered the folds of the corpse wrapping. There, it disappeared. It concealed itself from the pressure of the people and their insistence that it make the call to prayer.

If the One-Eyed Tigris resembled a city of ghosts on that day, it did not bother the scribes of the Overleaf Society. All of them assembled in their round boat: Ring Finger with a large notebook under his arm; Pinky with her daughter beside her; Middle Finger, who was stark naked and clapping. They were all escorting him to his wedding. Meanwhile, Thumb, whom I was seeing for the first time, was busy reading to the people in a resounding voice. Even though I did not see Pointer at that time, I felt as though I were seeing the whole society. Like the people, they were gripping their heads so they would preserve their names. Out of everyone that day, they were the bravest and most composed.

In their midst was a big chest made of gold, with silver tracery that looked like a sepulchre. It swayed and shook with the waves. It kept them from drowning, and they clung to it, pulling on the ropes that connected their waists and feet to it. The four handles of the sepulchre resembled pears, and ropes were tied to them. The idlers came down from the hill and gathered with their candles, their bowls, and their spoons. Energy was creeping into them. They beat their bowls, sang, and made fun of the people, all people. The people paid them no heed, focused as they were on getting home quickly amid the thick yellow air.

"Pinky, Ring Finger, Middle Finger, Thumb . . . Where's Pointer?" I was not the only one who had that question.

"Let's ask Khando," said Baghdadli as she turned right and left, only to find him underneath her, kissing her feet. The siblings reconciled faster than I had expected, but Khando was not aware of the boat of the scribes. Before long, an answer came from Thumb himself, his hand placed on the sepulchre.

"This is our holy Pointer, our martyr and our teacher." He pointed to the sepulchre as he spoke. The people laughed as they imagined a hand pointing with its pointer finger cut off. Pointer, the index finger of the society, was dead. But I did not laugh. Fear began welling up in my chest. I asked Baghdadli if we could start repeating our names so that we would not forget them, like some of the people. The names had started to vanish.

"The third chapter of our exercises, in the script of the holy Mazfur," continued Thumb, reading from his notebook, "Recollections, Events, and Incidents from the Past."

"In my hands are the exercises of my sons, the Overleaf Society, and the exercises of my teachers, of blessed memory. Under the shadow of their writings slept slaves' ideas and their magnificent thoughts.

"In the month of Rajab in the second year of the plague, at two o'clock in the afternoon, a dead tortoise, fifty cubits long, was discovered under a Hindu temple.

"On the following day, a strange red cloud appeared, followed by a heavy downpour. Tons of frogs rained down with it.

"In the month of Ramadan in the year following the Blessed Year, that is, one year after the passage of the flock of blessed ostriches that the French sultan sent the Turkish sultan, the workers of a French ship delivered a newspaper-printing press.

"Two hours after that, Madame Patricia disembarked from the same ship along with her Black serving girls. Accompanied by Father Emmo, she wandered among all the palaces lining the Shatt. Then they ate lunch in the company of the wool merchant, Davenport.

"Seven days later, Davenport was seen on a boat that looked like a serpent with one of the sheikhs from the lakes. The sheikh's slaves and water buffalo followed behind them, dragging a dozen earthenware pots dating back to Sumerian times. Davenport was carrying his blue sheep. It stood on its back legs, raising its front hooves to climb a tree.

"In the year called the Year of the Locust, the locusts attacked and ate the doors. The solution proposed by the judge was to open all the doors. Then the locusts achieved their desire, and they stopped gnawing on the doors and more. They were content to hang on the walls and sleep until they dried up, died, and fell of their own accord. In that year, the wali warned against counterfeit money and promised to throw in prison and fine anyone who circulated it," said Thumb, reading on behalf of the other fingers of the Overleaf Society.

His voice struck everyone as disturbing and frightening after we ran to the bank to hear him from the nearest point possible. We observed the stunned people staring at him, too, and listening closely to his words. They gobbled up his words as though searching through them to find their parents and family. Thumb continued reading assiduously. After he tired, he allowed Pinky to draw the notebook of writing exercises from his hand so that she might read in his place.

"In March of that year, a year and a half had gone by since the Blessed Year. The priest called Emmo was seen to alight from the ship that brought him from Europe with his wife, Gabriella, together with their son, Charlotte, with the amputated leg, which he is said to have lost after encountering pirates and being kidnapped with his father."

"She was a girl, you mule!" said Baghdadli, correcting them, but I didn't believe her. Even history thought I was a boy. I did not believe I was a girl, and I had not known that my leg was amputated on account of pirates. Instead, my father had given my leg an injection to treat me for an illness, and in his well-known stupidity, he committed a mistake. He used a dirty needle, the wound got infected, the rot spread, and he amputated the leg himself.

"Should I correct this scribe whore?" asked Baghdadli, ignoring me.

Pinky went on reading diligently. The handsome idler handed her a flask of water. She drank, spat it out into the Shatt, and went on reading. Perhaps she said everything. Then the crowd started breaking up. Some of them were restless. Some of them went off to pee or to fetch their families. Meanwhile, the yellowness and the noise intensified. So did the fear.

"And this was my exercise from a few days ago: Charlotte, the son of Father Emmo, went out to the lakes and was lost there. People sent Shathra, the guide for the lost, to search for him. And when she brought him back, her father had gone missing too. It is said that this priest, Emmo, was seen telling the fishermen a handful of stories. Then they asked him about the Day of Resurrection, the Great Assembly. They were on the Shatt and having a good time with him, and he was laughing and taking his ease with them. But the three came out of the river and vanished towards the other bank."

After removing her bandages, Rahlo joined the crowd of people. She patted their shoulders and asked to be shown the way. We had our eyes on her, but then we lost her. We looked for her everywhere. A moment came when I could not find her beside our group; I wanted to scream her name and put people to work in searching for her. But then her voice interrupted my curiosity.

"I don't remember my name. My name! Does anyone know my name?" cried Rahlo. She wandered among the people, asking them. We thought she was concealing some judgment or speaking fragmentary words so we would listen to her, the way that blind beggars call out in the city. They say something that brings you to a halt by puzzling your mind. Then they fall silent so you listen to them. They detain you in order to beg from you.

"Your name is Rahlo," I told her. Baghdadli told her that her name was Rahlo. It was the last moment of that day that I remembered my name, and Rahlo's name and Baghdadli's. I forgot them all. Even

Khando forgot his name. The people stopped listening to the Overleaf Society since it was no longer useful in the least. How could you distinguish your family's story or your own in the exercises of the Overleaf Society if you did not know your name?

After having congregated in the form of tight circles, the people all dispersed and became fragmented. No one knew anyone's name. It became obvious that the Day of Resurrection was beginning from that moment, for as it was said, one of the signs of that day was a man would be stupefied and forget his own name.

No one knew my name. No one seemed to want to ask about my name. I didn't know the color of the sky or the air around us at that time. We were in the blackness of nonexistence. The strangers, however, those staying at the hospital, were luckier than we, less in need of their names than we. The sun wanted to set and leave us. It went down into the piggy bank. A voice was rising and coming toward us. It resembled the quick panting of a wolf. It was the people, including the Zurkhaneh Lion, crying out, "No one knows my name." Rahlo, who was the first of us to forget her name, was not the only one. Meanwhile, the Overleaf Society was in the heart of the One-Eyed Tigris, reading history without pause. They were reciting the days with great zeal, as though playing a rural tune, even though no one was listening to them. The people dispersed and left the bank, searching for their names.

"Go down to the river," I heard a voice cry.

I went down to the river without ascertaining the identity of the speaker. I went down to the river, and the river knew my name. *I am Charlotte.* I remembered that when I immersed myself entirely in the water and then raised my head out of the water to breathe. Father Emmo stood leaning against a rock two meters away from the Overleaf Society's boat. Everyone learned the trick. They threw themselves into the river and came out with their names, remembering them once again. The river knew all the names. My father repeated exactly what the Overleaf Society had narrated. The yellowness was dying out; the sun was setting. There was no fog. The birds began soaring through the air once again.

"I was preaching to two friends among the fishermen. They asked me about the Day of Resurrection. That happened around two weeks ago, or maybe less, on the day that I disappeared. They appeared to be deeply affected by what I told them of that awful day. I cried and embraced them. We left the river on the far bank. I intended to go to Quarantine Island, where one of the people quarantining asked me to pray for him since he was dying. But after the first step on dry land, we forgot our names, both I and the fishermen. The police of Quarantine Island came across us. We did not remember our names; we were unable to clarify our identities, our activities, and our families. No one recognized us, and it was as though we were without names. They held us captive on the island, and we stayed there for days until we heard about the Day of Resurrection, when everyone fled and there was a general madness. The army left their posts and their watchtowers, and we fled. I recovered my name as soon as I plunged into the river." When my father explained all that, he lifted me to his shoulder. I lay my head against that shoulder and felt myself sinking into his chest. His smell was exactly the same. I recalled the feeling of happiness that came over me when I lost him, but I felt no shame about it, even as it left me. What I felt was a sense of safety so deep it was as if I never had been safe before.

At the end of that day, the dust dissipated and the sun appeared, naked of clouds. Everyone gestured toward it as though they were observing the sun for the first time in their lives. The Day of Resurrection had ended—or it had been delayed, I don't know which. More than half a century has passed, and nothing has happened yet. Things have happened, both marvelous and terrible, but the heavenly trumpet has not yet sounded, even when people brought Finjan, carried on a bier.

We have not heard a melody presented by the sky. Some people thought, including Baghdadli, that the wailing of his mother coming from below, even though we were not on the upper floor, was the angry voice of the angels being led by Jesus. But the plain sight of Finjan's mother as she conducted the funeral rites for slain children cleared away those doubts.

I saw the parrot emerge from the folds of the corpse. Dear God! The corpse that I saw the parrot enter several hours earlier had been the corpse of Finjan. The parrot left the shoulder of the Zurkhaneh Lion so that the blackened corpse of Finjan could take its place.

During the early hours on the Day of Resurrection, Finjan happened to pass by the shack of the fishermen. His six companions were among them. He ran toward them with a leather bag filled with oil on his back. He kicked open the door and sprawled out before them after igniting the oil. He wanted to burn them up, but they fled away. The skin on his back melted. He couldn't move, as the fire consumed him. The first time I heard his name in his mother's mouth, I asked myself why she would name her son *Finjan* if she loved him. Why would she call him by the word that means the cups used for drinking coffee and tea? My father, who wrapped his arms around me in a fierce embrace, was not one to let a question go. He explained to me later that Finjan's mother was like other women, fearing that the evil eye of envy might strike him, or he might get lost or suffer any of the other dangers of life on the water. People here call their children by ridiculous names, like Finjan (*cup*), or Zabala (*garbage*), Sahn (*plate*), Aamud (*pillar*), and Qitan (*thread*), believing that such names will ward off death and the anger, spears, and guns of the people. The more foolish the child's name, the higher his value in his parents' eyes and the greater their fear on his account. Yet that river made a mockery of their scheme, for the river erased all the names, both the foolish ones and the beautiful ones. We were all forgotten.

If you ever have forgotten your name, you begin to care less about forgetting it in your old age, which is what I am now starting to feel.

This is a story about children that was not made for children. Everything I experienced did not eliminate my old desire to leave home and live in nature, at peace with the monsters of the wild. It made that wish even stronger, and it was just one of many other adventures I went on to meet.

EPILOGUE

The four quarters of this story were sent to a magazine offering a debut-fiction competition for girls under the age of sixteen. Seeing as I am now fifteen-plus-sixty years old, I thought I would qualify by ignoring the sixty. After seven months, this response came back to me:

> Dear Charlotte,
> We are absolutely thrilled to inform you that your story, "Shathra," has not only been selected for the long list of our prize, but it has thoroughly captivated our attention with its truly unique qualities. Your exceptional work has left us breathless.
>
> We wholeheartedly invite you to join us in beautiful Boston to celebrate this remarkable achievement. It will be a splendid opportunity to meet with other talented authors, engage in inspiring conversations about books, and immerse ourselves in the boundless joys of storytelling.
>
> As we celebrate your remarkable talent, our editor has a suggestion. They firmly believe that your story will shine even brighter under the title "The River Knows My Name." This title beautifully encapsulates the essence of your work and is certain to strike a chord with readers.

Your unwavering dedication to your craft is indeed commendable, and we eagerly look forward to delving deeper into the captivating world you've crafted within your story. Once again, Charlotte, we extend our congratulations and express our heartfelt gratitude for sharing your extraordinary talent with us.

Warm regards,

The editors

ABOUT THE AUTHOR

Photo © 2023 MaryAnne Aberion

Mortada Gzar is an Iraqi American writer, filmmaker, visual artist, and political cartoonist. He is the author of the memoir *I'm in Seattle, Where Are You?*, which was long-listed for the PEN Translation Prize; four novels; a children's book; and a short-story collection. He has also illustrated two books for children and has had his work published in *Words Without Borders*, *World Literature Today*, and *Iraq + 100: The First Anthology of Science Fiction to Have Emerged from Iraq*, as well as numerous Arabic newspapers. Gzar is the creator of the Seattle Arab Film Festival, and his film *Language* was awarded a grant by the Doha Film Institute. He was born in Kuwait in 1982, grew up in Basra, Iraq, and now lives in Seattle, Washington. For more information, visit www.mortadagzar.co.

ABOUT THE TRANSLATOR

Luke Leafgren is an assistant dean of Harvard College, where he teaches courses on translation and serves as Allston Burr Resident Dean of Mather House. After growing up in northern Wisconsin as the child of a high school teacher and a sled dog racer, Leafgren received bachelor degrees at Columbia University and the University of Oxford before earning a PhD in comparative literature at Harvard University. Leafgren has published seven translations of Arabic novels. He received the 2018 Saif Ghobash Banipal Prize for Arabic Literary Translation for his rendering of Muhsin Al-Ramli's *The President's Gardens*, and his translation of Najwa Barakat's *Mister N* was a finalist for the 2023 EBRD Literature Prize and the winner of the 2023 Saif Ghobash Banipal Prize for Arabic Literary Translation.